"You're the father."

A wave of satisfaction swept over Del, catching him by surprise. He gave Libby a hug. Beneath his palms he could feel the delicate bones of her back.

Possessive tenderness poured through him, and words he'd never intended to say in his life sprang out of his mouth. "I'll marry you."

He clamped his lips shut. But after a moment of shock he found it felt right. Marriage—he'd never thought of it, but now… Yeah, that was the answer to the problem.

She wouldn't be on his mind so much if he married her.

Libby hadn't responded—overcome with gratitude, no doubt.

"I'll tell everyone that I'm the father and—"

"No!" Libby pushed free of his arms.

Del stared at her in surprise. "You want to tell them?"

"No! I mean I don't want anyone to know you're the father. Not ever!"

Dear Reader,

This month we've got two wonderful books about pregnant heroines. I've never been pregnant myself, but these writers made it easy for me to see myself in their heroines' places. And what crazy circumstances each one of them finds herself facing.

Alexandra Sellers' *Shotgun Wedding* introduces us to Carlee Miller, happily planning a life with her about-to-be child—until she discovers there was a mix-up at the sperm bank. And now millionaire dad-to-be Hal Ward wants in on the action. And not just the diaper-changing action, either. Once this guy sets eyes on the mother of his child, he's looking forward to making his next baby the old-fashioned way.

For Libby Sinclair, heroine of Sandra Paul's *Baby on the Way*, it was the old-fashioned way that got her into trouble in the first place. And now Del Delaney, the other half of that troublemaking night, is back in town—just in time to crash Libby's baby shower and let her know there will be *lots* of nights just like it in her future. And for some reason, Libby's not complaining!

Enjoy them both, then come back next month for two more Yours Truly novels, the books all about unexpectedly meeting, dating—and marrying!—Mr. Right.

Yours,

Leslie J. Wainger
Senior Editor and Editorial Coordinator

Please address questions and book requests to:
Silhouette Reader Service
U.S.: 3010 Walden Ave., P.O. Box 1325, Buffalo, NY 14269
Canadian: P.O. Box 609, Fort Erie, Ont. L2A 5X3

SANDRA PAUL

Baby on the Way

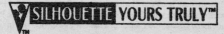

SILHOUETTE YOURS TRULY™

Published by Silhouette Books
America's Publisher of Contemporary Romance

To my dear cousin Betty Williams and
my dear brother-in-law Steve Douglas.
Thanks for all your help!

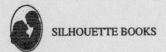

SILHOUETTE BOOKS

ISBN 0-373-52056-5

BABY ON THE WAY

Copyright © 1997 by Sandra Novy Chvostal

Printed in U.S.A.

A Letter From the Author

My husband is a real "tough" guy—a welder who never bothers to complain about the burning slivers of metal that sometimes become embedded beneath his skin while he's working. Yet he suffered along so convincingly with me during the labor of our first child that the nurses paid more attention to him than to me. (Much to my indignation!) I can still remember the wonder on his face when he first saw our son, and he soon became an expert at changing diapers and rocking the baby to sleep.

It was a good thing he did, because our next child arrived two months premature, and due to complications, I ended up spending a few days in intensive care. My husband took care of our new baby, spending hours in the preemie ward carefully cuddling our "baby doll"—a tiny, perfect little girl no bigger than the length of his callused hand.

A few years later, he was the first to hold our second daughter, too, and was so reluctant to hand his precious bundle over to "Mom" that I had to threaten to get up off the delivery bed and come get her—stitches or no stitches.

In *Baby on the Way*, Del isn't too sure at first how he feels when he learns Libby is expecting. But as soon as he holds his new little one in his arms, he's immediately smitten.

Yes, Del—like my husband—discovers that he really loves babies. After all, what true hero doesn't?

Books by Sandra Paul

Silhouette Yours Truly

Baby on the Way

Silhouette Romance

*You Are Invited
to a Baby Shower
For: Elizabeth Sinclair
Place: Susan Kayle's House
Time: 8 p.m., Friday Night
Shhhhh! It's a SURPRISE!*

"**D**el" A. Delaney paused in the act of chugging milk straight from the carton, his attention caught by the small pink card tossed carelessly atop the gift boxes on his sister's kitchen table. His gaze brushed over the coy stork posing with a blanketed blue bundle in its beak, and fastened on the name penned in below. Elizabeth. Elizabeth Sinclair.

Libby? His jaw clenched. *It couldn't be.*

Slamming the carton down, he snatched up the card. "Chris!" he shouted. "Christine Delaney! Get out here this minute."

"You bellowed, brother?" his sister asked, strolling into the kitchen. Her gaze—the same dark blue as his own—fell on the open carton of milk. Shaking her fashionably tousled dark hair in disapproval, she said, "Darn it, Del, if you don't use a glass I'm going to—"

"Never mind that." He thrust the card at her. "What the hell is this?"

Christine's slim brows lifted at his harsh tone. She took the card from him and studied it, pursing her lips thoughtfully. "I'm going to go out on a limb here and say it's an invitation for a baby shower—another term for a party celebrating the arrival of a small human being sometimes referred to as a B-A-B-Y."

"Damn it, I know what a baby is." Del snatched the card away. "Are you saying Libby is *pregnant?*"

Chris beamed, patting his arm. "You've finally got it. I always knew there was a glimmer of intelligence in there somewhere. Now step aside while I gather a few more things together. I told Susan I'd get there early and help with the decorating."

She bustled around, opening cupboards while Del stood frozen to the spot. "How far along is she?" he demanded.

"Hmm?"

Del glared at the back of his sister's head, resisting the urge to shake her. He spaced out each word. "I said, *how far along is she?*"

Christine glanced up. "Libby? About seven or eight months."

She turned away while Del, overcome with the urgent need to sit down, straddled a kitchen chair. He felt as if he'd been poleaxed, a familiar feeling he'd had once before: the first time he'd looked into Elizabeth Sinclair's startled brown eyes.

Seven and a half months ago.

"Where is she?" he growled.

"Still at work," Chris said, her voice muffled as

she burrowed in a cavernous cupboard. "I already told you that when you got here."

Yeah, Chris had told him. In fact, it was the first question he'd asked her when stepping into his family's Victorian house where Libby rented the third-floor rooms. Actually he'd known, even before Christine told him so, that Libby wasn't home. The big old house had an empty feeling.

His jaw clenched. Damn it, he should have called— he'd *planned* to call. Yet, it was precisely the strength of his need to do so that had kept him from picking up the phone. He stared down at the invitation in his hands. And now Libby was pregnant. He still couldn't quite believe it. The memory of slender white limbs and soft, slight curves floated through his mind.

"Now, Del. I know exactly what you're thinking."

His gaze whipped up, fastening on his sister. Christine was watching him as she sat back on her heels, cradling a large yellow bowl in her lap. "You do?" he said.

"Yep, I sure do." She nodded decisively, making her curls bounce. "You're thinking I made a big mistake, taking Libby on as a boarder—that she's some kind of irresponsible flake. But you're wrong. She's not like that at all. Once you meet her, I know you'll see right away Libby is a good person. Why, everyone in the town loves her. Even Mrs. Peyton says..."

Christine chattered on, while Del's frowning gaze returned to the paper. So Libby hadn't told anyone about him...about *them*.

"...and with all the traveling I do for my job, and all the traveling you do for yours..."

But why not? She had to know they'd find out sometime.

"...this house sits empty ten months out of the year, anyway. It's nice to have someone who'll be here all the time..."

He'd left her an emergency number. Why hadn't she used it? Unless...his brows drew together as his initial certainty about the baby's paternity wavered. "Who's the father?" he asked abruptly.

"With Libby here—" Thrown off stride by the interruption, Chris paused, her brows drawing together in puzzlement. "What?"

"Who does Libby say is the father of her baby?"

"Oh. No one." Seeing her brother's darkening frown, Chris added hastily, "I'm not kidding. I know it sounds strange, but she's honestly never said. Half the town believes she must have been pregnant before she arrived in Lone Oak, while the other half suspects the father might be the new doctor over in Vicksville." She lowered her voice confidentially. "He's a real babe and I guess Libby's been seen with him a time or two."

Del's eyes narrowed. "Oh, she has, has she? This...doctor," he drawled. "He comes here to see her?"

Chris shook her head again. "No, not that I'm aware of. And Libby doesn't ever talk about him, which is part of the reason I don't think it's him." She rose gracefully to her feet. Stacking the bowl in a carton next to the gifts, she added, "Besides, he seems like a nice guy. Certainly not the type to get a woman pregnant and then abandon her."

Del straightened, a flush burning along his cheekbones, his fingers crushing the card in his fist. "Is that what Libby told you?" he demanded. "That some guy *abandoned* her?"

Chris picked up her box. "No, that's just my theory. I told you Libby's never said a word and I don't have the nerve to press her. She's sweet and all, but kind of...reserved, if you know what I mean?"

"No," Del said bluntly. "I don't." The Libby he knew—the Libby he'd gotten to know very well indeed during the three days they'd been snowbound here alone together—hadn't been reserved. Oh, she'd been aloof at first and a little shy at times, but mainly she'd been warm, and giving, and honest. At least he'd *thought* she'd been honest.

Pushing back his chair, he stood abruptly and lifted the box from Christine's arms.

"What are you doing? Where are you going with that?" she demanded as he headed to the door.

"To the baby shower, of course," he said without pausing. "To meet this brave, sweet, silent paragon you keep talking about. I have a feeling," he added grimly, "that this meeting is long overdue."

"Surprise!"

Libby jumped, her hands flying up instinctively to cover the rounded mound of her abdomen as Susan Kayle's door flew open. Behind the blonde crowded a group of smiling women while across a far wall a blue banner declared Congratulations, Libby, On Your Pending Arrival.

Libby's throat tightened. A surprise shower. They'd given her a surprise shower. "Oh, this is just too much," she said helplessly. They were all so sweet.

So excited. A tenseness she hadn't even been aware of eased within her chest, leaving her ridiculously close to tears.

As if on cue, Susan strode forward, plucking off Libby's damp rain hat and divesting her of her purse and coat with the ease of an experienced hostess. "I swear, these Oregon summer rains get worse every year," she said. Expertly, she ushered Libby forward to a huge, overstuffed white armchair. "Now, just sit down and catch your breath a minute. As usual, Christine is late and we can't get started without her."

Libby sat down. Way down. The cushions sank beneath her weight until she felt as if she were enveloped by a giant marshmallow. Folds of her denim jumper bunched beneath her hips, constricting the heavy material across her stomach. She shifted, trying to rearrange the material while she glanced around at the women chattering in groups. The warmth of belonging stole over her.

In Beverly Hills, California, where she had grown up, Libby had never known many of her mother's neighbors. Thick walls separated her mother's minimansion from the properties around her, and even more isolating had been Liz's dislike of mingling with "outsiders"—meaning anyone who didn't share her all-consuming interest in the movie industry. Since Libby planned to be a teacher, and her interest in the film world her mother loved had been tepid at best, she'd often felt like an outsider, too.

Until she'd come to Lone Oak. This was the kind of small town she'd always longed to live in, a place filled with "real" people who cared about one another.

"So, were you surprised, Libby? Did you really believe Susan was just having a Tupperware party?" Anabel Royce demanded.

Libby abandoned the battle with her skirt to answer the slim brunette. "I was completely surprised."

"And didn't you think it was odd I made you work overtime at the store tonight after you'd asked for the evening off?"

"I certainly did." But she really hadn't found it surprising at all. Anabel, who had hired her to clerk at the department store, hadn't been pleased when her new help had turned up pregnant after only a couple of months on the job. Libby had assumed tonight's overtime was simply an expression of her boss's displeasure. She'd been doubly sure of it when Anabel had arranged for old Bill, one of the janitorial staff, to drop her off at the party instead of waiting for Libby herself.

How wrong she'd been—how wrong about them all. She'd expected the whole town to turn its back on her once everyone discovered she was single and pregnant with no sign of the baby's father in sight. Instead, they'd all been more than kind, not even questioning her about the baby's father once they learned—via Christine—that she preferred not to talk about him.

"Did you hear we'll be having a sale in the infants' department this week?" Brooke Frenzel asked softly, and Libby brushed a strand of rain-damp hair off her cheek, turning to smile up at the younger woman perched on the arm of her chair. Brooke worked in the store, too, and as soon as she'd learned Libby was expecting, she'd made it her business to keep her informed of upcoming sales. "They have some darling outfits discounted," Brooke added.

Libby's mouth turned down ruefully. "I think I'd better stock up on the more practical stuff like diapers."

"But, Libby, your baby can't run around in diapers all the time," Anabel said, smoothing her designer dress. She lowered her voice. "I might be able to increase your employee discount some. The right clothes are so important."

Not to a child they aren't, Libby thought. She'd had plenty of the "right" clothes growing up—and all she'd craved was love. Still, how kind of Anabel to worry about it. She smiled up at the woman, saying, "Thanks, Anabel, but once my mother hears about the baby, I'm sure I'll have more outfits than the baby could ever wear."

"Why, Elizabeth Sinclair, you told me two weeks ago you planned on telling your mother about the baby immediately. You mean you still haven't done it yet?" a shrill voice inquired.

Her mother wasn't the only one she hadn't told, Libby thought involuntarily. For a moment, a pair of piercing blue eyes flashed in her mind.

She blinked, dispelling the vision as Brooke whispered, "Uh-oh, you're in for it now. Lone Oak's most notorious busybody is headed this way."

Libby looked up to find Pamela Peyton—with her plump shadow of a daughter, Dorrie Jean, in tow—elbowing her way toward Libby's chair. Libby said admonishingly, "C'mon, Brooke, she's not that bad."

"No, she just can't understand that not everyone wants her advice on their private business," her friend whispered, and moved discreetly away as the pair approached. The other women standing nearby followed suit and, cowardly, Libby wished she could escape also. Not that she disliked Mrs. Peyton, she assured herself hastily. It was just that she received a lecture from Christine's nearest neighbor every time they met, her attempts to avoid the older woman meeting with no success. Libby *always* got caught.

She smiled bravely at the two women as Mrs. Peyton planted her stout body in front of her while Dorrie Jean hovered timidly in the background. The matron's pointed nose seemed to quiver in her round face as she declared, "Goodness gracious, Elizabeth. I'd let my Dorrie Jean know a thing or two if she didn't tell me the moment she was expecting."

"Mother..." Dorrie, blushing fiery red, plucked fruitlessly at her mother's sleeve.

Mrs. Peyton shrugged her off. "Now, Dorrie Jean, Libby knows I always speak my mind..."

Yes, Libby certainly knew that—Pamela Peyton had a reputation for speaking her mind to anyone who would listen.

"...and I think her mother will be disappointed she wasn't told sooner." Mrs. Peyton turned back to Libby. "Don't you agree?" she demanded.

"I don't think my mother and I have the same kind of relationship as you and Dorrie," Libby admitted. In fact, she was sure of it. Mrs. Peyton kept tabs on every move her poor daughter made. Libby hadn't spoken to her mother since she'd moved to Lone Oak.

Mrs. Peyton persisted. "Still, not telling her must worry you..."

Not telling Liz Sinclair was the least of Libby's

worries. Not telling the baby's father—now *that* was another story.

"In fact, a girl's mother should be the first to know..."

Libby shifted uncomfortably. Maybe she should have told *him*—first thing.

"She might be shocked..."

He'd be stunned.

"...and maybe a little upset..."

Furious was more like it.

"...but I'm sure she won't blame you..."

Maybe he wouldn't—at least not completely. The problem was she really didn't know him well enough to predict *how* he'd react. All she knew was that he had no interest in settling down—in Lone Oak or anywhere else—and certainly no intention of getting married. He'd made that clear enough.

Mrs. Peyton leaned closer. "Tell her, Elizabeth. Tell her right away and get it over with."

Should she tell him? His strong, determined face flashed through her mind. *I never stay in one place too long—my job keeps me constantly on the move.* The memory of his words banished her doubts. At least her own father, the first of Liz's three "ex's," had been close enough to visit occasionally.

No, she'd made the right decision. She didn't want her baby growing up with a father who didn't care, who showed up only one or two weeks out of the year. Besides, he certainly hadn't made much of an effort to keep in touch. Sure, he'd left her an emergency number, but he certainly hadn't bothered to call. Smoothing down her jumper over her stomach, Libby unconsciously lifted her chin. As far as she was concerned, *he* no longer had anything to do with the matter. Having this baby was her decision, and hers alone.

Mrs. Peyton patted her arm. "I can see that you realize I'm right," she said with all the assurance of a woman who couldn't imagine ever being wrong.

Libby dredged up a smile. "Thank you, Mrs. Peyton," she said, avoiding a direct answer. "You've been a great help."

Looking satisfied, Mrs. Peyton allowed her daughter to lead her away to the refreshment table as the doorbell chimed again.

Susan hurried in from the kitchen. "That has to be Christine," she said, striding toward the door. Glancing at Libby, her eyebrows rose. "Good Lord, you look tense, Libby! This is supposed to be fun, for goodness' sake. Try and relax a little. Lean back and take a deep breath."

Obediently, Libby leaned back and took a deep breath—then promptly lost it again. Christine entered the hallway, and right behind her Libby glimpsed a man with dark rumpled hair, wearing jeans and a flannel shirt.

A tall, broad-shouldered man. A slim-hipped, sexy man. A very grim-faced man.

"Del" A. Delaney.

2

What was *he* doing here?

Frantically, Libby tried to extricate herself from the chair. Del hadn't seen her yet; Susan had claimed his attention from the moment he'd stepped in the hallway. If she could only hoist herself up, there was a slim chance she could escape to the bathroom before he caught sight of her.

But the chair wouldn't let her go, and across the room she could hear Chris's voice lilting above the buzz of feminine greetings, "So where is she? Where's Libby?"

Libby stifled a groan as, without hesitation, Del looked up over Susan's blond head, his dark blue gaze snaring Libby's as she collapsed back in her chair. She was thankful to be sitting down, because she suddenly felt light-headed. In all her fantasies of seeing Del again, she'd been poised, slim and flawlessly groomed. In control and coldly aloof. Never had she imagined confronting him after a hard day's work with her hair all wet from the rain, her makeup worn off and her ankles swollen to the size of tree trunks.

And with the leading ladies of Lone Oak curiously watching.

Sure enough, Christine—like several others—had followed her brother's gaze. "There you are!" she sang out. Grabbing Del's arm, she pulled him away from Susan and toward Libby, all the while chattering gaily to the other guests. "Hi, everyone! Guess what? Del's back! He's just finished up a job in Seoul and decided to drop in and visit the old family home. He insisted on coming with me—supposedly to help with the decorations, but in reality, I suspect, to get a piece of cake."

Everyone accepted the explanation easily enough, Libby noticed. Susan even took the opportunity to call out after him, "Oh, do you like sweet things?" batting her lashes in a way that made Libby's stomach turn with a nausea that had become all too familiar during the past few months. Personally, she didn't buy the explanation for a moment. Did he suspect...? Surely not.

Still, her trepidation grew when he nodded slightly in response to Susan's remark, but didn't pause or remove his gaze from Libby as he made his way across the room behind his sister. He reached her side and Libby swallowed, painfully aware of that laser-sharp gaze sweeping slowly over her face to her swollen breasts, and down farther yet, to linger on her rounded belly. Oh, he suspected all right.

She avoided his eyes as he looked back up to her face, focusing instead on Christine, who'd plopped down on the arm of the chair.

"Sorry I'm late, Lib," Chris said cheerfully. Her mobile mouth turned down in a wry grimace, as she playfully elbowed the tall figure standing silently beside her. "I'd blame Del here, but I doubt anyone would believe me. Oh, this is my big brother, Del. Del, this is Libby—our boarder. I'm so happy you both finally have the chance to meet.''

To Libby, the silence that followed seemed to stretch forever. Finally Del drawled, ''Hello… Libby, is it?''

She nodded, sighing in relief that he hadn't revealed that they knew each other. Maybe he wasn't as angry as she'd first imagined?

Hopefully, her gaze lifted to his…and skittered away again. His hard face wore a politely inquiring expression, but his eyes—oh, those eyes! Accusing anger lit them like a hot blue flame.

She could feel the heat of a blush rise in her cheeks. He might suspect but he couldn't know for sure, she reminded herself frantically. All she had to do was to act natural.

But acting natural suddenly seemed very hard to do. Her throat closed tight and her hands displayed an alarming tendency to flutter. Resolutely, she clasped them tightly in her lap. ''Hello,'' she managed to say, forcing a smile. ''Christine has told me a lot about you.''

She had no intention of shaking hands, but he reached down, his knuckles almost brushing her stomach as he captured her cold fingers. ''Oh, she has, has she?'' he said. ''Funny, she hasn't said much about you. In fact, until today I had no idea at all that our new little boarder was expecting.''

''Oh, didn't you?'' Libby said weakly. The rough texture of his hand felt disconcertingly familiar. Suddenly she remembered the last time he'd touched her—touched her all over. His fingers molding her breasts, gliding down between her thighs. Her fingers burned in his big, warm grasp and, unobtrusively, she tried to tug her hand free.

Del, however, ignored her efforts, his grip tightening as she continued to avoid his gaze. She finally abandoned the hand-to-hand combat to remark, "Maybe Christine didn't think you'd be interested in babies."

He leaned closer, his expression darkening. Libby shrank back into the cushions, alarmed at having provoked him as he said, "Then *maybe* she'd be wrong, wouldn't she? I am *very* interested in *your* baby."

Chris glanced back and forth between them and beamed. "I just knew you two would hit it off," she said happily. "It's almost uncanny, this ability I have to read people. Didn't I tell you, Libby, that my brother was a great guy?"

"Yes, you did." Libby gave another tug on her hand.

"Del!" Mrs. Peyton, pulling a red-faced Dorrie Jean behind her, joined the group. With a warning squeeze, Del released Libby to smile briefly down at the older woman.

"How are you?" Mrs. Peyton said, her broad smile making her cheeks look plumper than ever. "I hear congratulations are in order..."

The room blurred before Libby's eyes, clearing again as Mrs. Peyton continued, "...that you got another promotion."

"Thanks, yes, I did," Del answered.

"Dorrie Jean and I can't wait to hear all about it." Mrs. Peyton released Dorrie Jean to pull a chair closer, but before she could sit down, Del glanced across the room and said casually, "It looks like Susan is cutting the cake."

"She is?" Mrs. Peyton's eyes sharpened with interest. "She'll probably want my help. Don't worry, I'll be right back."

She hurried off with Dorrie Jean following and Chris bent over to whisper in Libby's ear, "Mrs. P. is dedicated to finding a husband for Dorrie Jean and thinks Del would be perfect. She asks about him every time I talk to her even though I've told her over and over that this brother of mine is married to his work—"

"Chris…" Del's low voice interrupted his sister's and he shot her a warning glare. She glanced inquiringly up at him. "I've told you before. Quit discussing my business with everyone in Lone Oak."

"I don't," Chris declared indignantly. "I'm merely polite when Mrs. Peyton asks about you, that's all. It's not my fault she thinks you'd be the perfect son-in-law."

Obviously unconvinced, he turned back to Libby. Studying her with intent eyes, he demanded, "And what exactly has Chris told you about me?"

"Well, she said…" Libby groped for a coherent answer. What *had* Chris told her—and what had she learned from Del himself? She couldn't seem to think straight. He was standing so close that she could feel the cold, crisp air from outside that still clung to him, see the tiny lines that fanned out from the corners of his eyes.

"Are you all right, Libby?" Chris asked.

Libby blinked. Chris was staring at her in concern, while Del's gaze held narrow-eyed speculation. Anxious to distract him, Libby hurried into speech. "She told me about your promotion—and what a lot of responsibility you have now. I suppose you have to get back right away," she added on a hopeful note.

He obviously didn't appreciate her attempt to hurry him off. Crossing his arms, he drawled, "Actually, no. I plan to spend a few days in Lone Oak. Look up an old...acquaintance I met on my last visit."

"Oh?"

"Oh, *yes.*" His wide mouth tightened as he studied her face. "By the way, Chris wasn't sure...when *is* your baby due?"

Libby hesitated, floundering through mental math. She stammered out, "In...in about another three months."

Christine's eyebrows lifted in surprise. "But, Lib, I thought you said—"

"Excuse me, Chris, but Susan is trying to get your attention—and Del's, too, I think," Libby said desperately. She gestured to the far side of the room. "I suppose she wants to start some games."

"The games!" Christine's blue eyes lit up. "I'm in charge of those." She hurried over to where the blonde stood waiting.

Libby held her breath, but to her dismay Del didn't follow his sister. Lifting his eyebrows in a sardonic fashion, he murmured, "Did you really think you could get rid of me that easily?" and casually appropriated the chair arm Christine had abandoned. "If you don't mind, I think I'll sit here," he said.

"I don't mind at all," Libby said, ignoring the way her heart thudded and her stomach twisted at his nearness. But she did mind because, for the minute, they were virtually alone. The last thing she wanted was for him to have the opportunity to ask more questions.

Sure enough, he leaned closer saying, "Three months to go, hmm? Why are they throwing you the shower so soon?"

"Christine thought it would be a good idea. That way, after I see what gifts I'm given, I'll know what I still need and can get prepared well ahead of time," Libby said quickly.

"That's a good answer," he said, a false note of admiration in his voice. "But are you sure you're not making a mistake about that date?"

Feigning surprise at the question, Libby forced herself to meet his gaze. "Of course I'm sure."

"I see." His eyes held a hard glint that made her pulse accelerate. "So you're saying that a few weeks after beginning an affair with me, you jumped into bed with someone else?"

"I'm not saying anything at all," Libby said, ignoring the way her heart pounded. Summoning up her courage, she added, "I really don't think it's any of your business."

Temper flared in his blue eyes again. "*Isn't* it?"

"Susan isn't cutting the cake yet. She told Mother she wants to wait," Dorrie Jean announced from behind them.

Libby jumped, but when she glanced up, Dorrie showed no sign of having overheard anything. She probably hadn't, Libby decided, breathing a sigh of relief. Del had kept his voice low, and the sounds of the women chattering nearby had most likely drowned him out. She turned away from him, seizing the distraction offered by Mrs. Peyton's return as the older woman sat next to Dorrie.

She could feel Del staring at her averted profile while he sat silently beside her—trying to unnerve her, no doubt. She gritted her teeth. Well, it wouldn't work. He might suspect she wasn't telling the truth but unless she admitted it, there was no way he could know for sure. She carefully avoided looking at him, listening with pretended absorption as Mrs. Peyton instructed everyone within hearing distance on the correct way to make a double-fudge cake.

"Three eggs are much better than two..."

More wasn't always better. Two could even be too much if one of the persons was domineering and unpredictable, here today and gone tomorrow—like Del.

"If you beat it too much, the cake won't rise..."

Her color rose under his narrow-eyed stare. Her senses felt overly heightened; she was aware of every breath Del took, every time he shifted the least little bit. He stretched out his legs and her glance fell on his big work boots—worn and scuffed at the toes. She'd never seen those boots before. She bit back a hysterical laugh. Suddenly, it seemed very funny to think she knew what his bare feet looked like but she'd never seen his shoes.

"The oven has to be set at precisely three hundred and fifty degrees. No hotter..."

Goodness, it was hot. Libby fanned herself with her hand. Del was sitting on the chair arm, with his arm slung along the back. She could feel the heat emanating from his virile body. He shifted a little closer and her nose twitched. She caught the familiar scent of fresh air, soap and Del. An unexpected ache bloomed in her chest. For days after he'd left, she'd breathed in his scent as it lingered on her pillows, feeling lonelier than she'd ever felt in her life...

"And there you have it! Perfect every time!"

It *had* been perfect—the first time they'd made love and even the second. Impossibly perfect. What a fool she'd been. How could she have gone to bed with a man she'd known only three days? Smiling and nodding as Mrs. Peyton finished her recital on a triumphant note, Libby rested her hand comfortingly on her abdomen. Still, at least now she'd never be lonely. She had her baby, good friends and a place she belonged. She didn't need anything else. Del had taken himself out of her life, and there he would stay.

She fought to ignore him, turning to laugh and joke with Christine as she came around to distribute small notepads and pencils for the first game. When Christine moved on, Libby immediately joined in with everyone else listing baby items to match the letters in the alphabet, trying to hide the fact that her fingers trembled around her pencil.

She breathed a sigh of relief as the game ended without incident. Maybe Del had gotten the message; maybe he was relieved to know she wasn't going to involve him with the baby. At any rate, if he was going to make a scene, surely he would have done so already. She glanced at him from the corner of her eye— a task made infinitely easier by the fact that Susan had strolled up to claim his attention. No doubt about it, his presence definitely livened up the party. Whenever the single women spoke to him, their voices lowered in unconscious invitation while even the married women's gazes rested on him more than they should.

Mrs. Peyton, glaring at Susan, kept pushing Dorrie Jean so close to him that at one point the poor girl almost fell in his lap. But despite all the attention and Libby's silent urging, Del never moved from her side.

"Don't you think we should have cake now?" Mrs. Peyton asked finally, apparently disgruntled at Dorrie Jean's lack of progress. With a small smile at Del, Susan took the hint and left to dispense the refreshments.

Mrs. Peyton finished hers off in record time, then watched disapprovingly as Libby pushed the thick pink icing off her piece before taking a few small bites. "Don't tell me you're dieting, Elizabeth," she said disapprovingly. "Why, when a woman is carrying a child, it's no time to worry about vanity."

Libby felt Del glance sharply down at her. Her hand shook. Icing fell from her plate, landing on the curve of her breast. Aware her cheeks were reddening again, she dabbed at the pink blob on the denim with her napkin, saying, "I'm not dieting, Mrs. Peyton."

"Good. Heaven knows, you're a skinny little thing. Hard enough going through this all alone, without getting sick, too."

"I'm not sick."

Mrs. Peyton ignored the comment. "So what are you going to have? A boy or a girl?"

"A boy, I think."

"You think?" Mrs. Peyton frowned. "Don't you know? I thought you were going to have a—what are those things called, Dorrie Jean? An ultrasound? You said the doctor had arranged for you to have one last week."

Aware of Del's intent interest, Libby said hastily,

"No, we decided I didn't need it. Wouldn't you like another piece of cake, Mrs. Peyton?"

The older woman looked tempted, but resolutely refused the bait. "Thank you, but no. That pink icing gives me gas."

"Mother!" Dorrie whispered in an agonized voice.

Mrs. Peyton faced her daughter. "Now, Dorrie Jean, there's nothing wrong with a little plain speaking." She turned back to frown at Libby's stomach, narrowing her eyes. "I'm not so sure it's a boy. You're not very big. Looks like a girl to me."

"I agree," Del drawled. He slanted a smile at Mrs. Peyton, who beamed back.

Libby shot him an angry glance. "Well, I think it's a boy."

"So do I," Christine agreed as she walked up. "It's a well-known fact that if you're carrying out front like Libby, then the baby is a boy."

"But she's shaped like a basketball—which means a girl," Mrs. Peyton argued stubbornly. "Boys are football shaped."

"But she's carrying low," Christine stated. "It has to be a boy."

Before Mrs. Peyton could counter again, Dorrie interposed quietly, "What are you going to name him, Libby?"

"I'm not sure yet..."

"Aren't you going to name the baby after the father?" Del asked, lifting his eyebrows in assumed surprise.

Libby stiffened. "No."

"Why not?" Del deftly dodged his sister's elbow, without removing his gaze from Libby's.

Because I don't know his father's name—only his nickname, Libby was tempted to reply. The father didn't stay around long enough to tell me his *real* first name.

She gave him a futile glare, relieved when Christine inadvertently interrupted the silent stare down. "Come on, guys. There's one more game," Chris said. She swept up a ball of yarn and attracted the crowd's attention, instructing, "Everyone cut off a piece of string. The one who comes closest to the size of Libby's waistline wins."

Libby wrenched her gaze from Del's. A lump had formed in her throat and she swallowed past the ache, smiling as Brooke came up to try her luck. *He doesn't know,* Libby reminded herself forcefully, lifting her arms and sitting forward as Brooke encircled her waist. He *can't* know for sure.

Her tension increased, however, tightening her muscles. She felt like a wooden doll as the women took turns measuring their yarn lengths around her, and she stiffened even more when Del suddenly said, "Give me a piece. I think I can win this one."

"You?" Christine hooted. "That dress you bought me last Christmas was so big, I could have fit in it twice. You're the worst judge of a woman's size I've ever seen."

The rest of the women joined in, teasing Del as he demanded the yarn from Christine and made a production of eyeing Libby. Despite all the laughter, the glint in his eye caused her heart to beat faster again and her stomach to churn. Finally, Del lopped off a piece the women all declared was much too small.

"It's apparent you don't know her very well," Mrs. Peyton chortled.

"Let's see," he replied.

He knelt by Libby's side and her breath caught. He was so near she could see the small dark specks in his deep blue eyes as his arms moved slowly around her. She held her breath. His hands brushed along her sides to her back and around to the front again. Both his palms pressed firmly against the hard, warm mound of her stomach as he pulled the yarn taut.

"Look at that," Christine said in surprise. "The yarn is exactly right."

Inside Libby's womb, the baby gave a lazy turn. Del's eyes widened in surprise, his pupils expanding until only a thin circle of blue remained. Then his expression altered.

His gaze locked with hers. Libby's stomach lurched at the hard certainty on his face. *He knows,* she finally admitted to herself. *He knows the baby is his.*

As if from a distance, she heard Mrs. Peyton's disappointed voice. "Darn it, I was close but it looks like Del wins the prize."

Libby clapped her hand over her mouth. Oh, good Lord. She was going to be sick.

3

Panicked, she pushed Del out of the way. *Oh, please, don't let me be sick here!* she prayed silently as she struggled to lever herself up from the chair. *Not on Susan's new blue Berber carpet. Not in the middle of my shower. Most of all, not in front of Del Delaney!*

A strong tanned hand suddenly caught hers, pulling her to her feet.

With a muffled, "Thank you," she skirted around Del's big body and hurried to Susan's bathroom.

Del was standing by the door when she finally came out—the same way he'd been waiting outside the bathroom at home the first time she'd met him. A rare blizzard had struck the state, resulting in a not-so-rare blackout as sleet coated the electrical lines causing a power failure. Before leaving on a buying trip, Christine had forewarned Libby about the problem and Libby had been prepared, arming herself with a flashlight before going in for her bath. When she'd emerged half an hour later, clad only in a man's shirt with the flashlight in hand, her heart had jumped at the unexpected sight of the big, masculine frame caught in the wavering beam.

"I'm sorry, I didn't mean to startle you. I'm Del—

Christine's brother,'' he'd said immediately, and her panic had subsided.

She wasn't startled to see him this time—there was no blackout and Susan's hallway was brightly lit—but her heart leapt in an oddly similar way as he straightened from where he'd been leaning against the jamb.

"Were you ill?" he asked.

She shook her head wearily. "No. I just needed to splash some cold water on my face."

Del eyed her critically. She still looked upset, and her hair was kind of sticking up on one side, but he decided she looked immeasurably better than she had before. He'd noticed immediately upon entering Susan's house how much more fragile Libby looked now. Faint shadows lingered beneath her soft brown eyes and, despite the hectic spots of color in her cheeks, she looked paler. She was thinner, too—his eyes swept lower—except, of course, for the added fullness to her small breasts and the surprising round ball of her belly.

His eyes lingered on that intriguing roundness and he had the urge to touch her again, to run his hands over her and explore her new fullness for himself. He straightened, impatient to get her alone.

"Well, then, let's go," he said, taking a step toward her. "Smile and say goodbye to everyone, but don't stop to talk or we won't get out of here for another two hours."

Not giving her a chance to protest, he took her arm, towing her behind him into the living room. The women immediately flocked their way, but Del refused to release his grip on Libby as sympathetic murmurings rose around them.

"You poor thing," Susan exclaimed.

Mrs. Peyton declared darkly, "Morning sickness—especially in the evening—is the pits."

"Are you all right, Libby?" Christine asked, her expression concerned.

Libby smiled wanly at her and the other women. "I'm fine. Just a little tired."

"You aren't leaving, are you?" Anabel said as Del led Libby to the door. "You haven't opened your presents yet."

Before Libby could answer, Del said firmly, "She's exhausted and wants to go home and rest. I've said I'll drive her."

He glanced at his sister, reading the surprise in her eyes. To forestall her from accompanying them or offering to take Libby herself, he added pointedly, "I knew you'd want to help Susan clean up and gather Libby's gifts together, Chris."

Christine said politely, if unenthusiastically, "Of course I'll help Susan." She glanced back at Libby. "But are you sure you don't want me to go with you?"

Del's grip on Libby's arm tightened fractionally, and she shook her head. "I'll be fine, but thank you—thank you all. This shower was such a wonderful surprise."

"Oh, pshaw," said Mrs. Peyton. "You just get on out of here and lie down. You're sleeping for two now, you know."

Amid the laughter and final farewells, Del slung his jacket around Libby's shoulders and hustled her out the door. The light mist was still falling, slickening the walkway from Susan's house, but although he kept a firm grip on Libby's arm to insure she didn't fall, Del didn't slacken his pace until they reached the sidewalk.

There, however, beneath the shelter of a huge, old oak growing in the parkway, he paused and turned her to face him, thankful to be away from the other women and finally alone with Libby.

The rain had dampened her brown hair to a dark chestnut. When he'd first met her, her hair had curved gently along her jaw. Now, it fell to her shoulders in a silky brown curtain, half hiding her face as she glanced away from him. Feathery strands clung to her pale cheeks and tiny diamond drops misted her dark lashes. He gently touched her cheek and she glanced up at him. Her soft brown eyes held a wary expression and he did what he'd longed to do from the first moment of seeing her huddled in that chair. Reaching out he put his hand firmly on her belly again. "It's mine," he said. "This is my baby."

His tone brooked no argument and he could see, once again, the helpless acknowledgment of his claim in her soft brown eyes. Then her mouth firmed and she stepped away. "This baby is none of your business."

Something inside him flared in angry denial at her words. His jaw set. "When we made love, everything about you became my business."

"Why? Because I'm pregnant?" She held his gaze steadily. "You made love with other women and moved on. What makes me so special?"

He didn't know, but she was. The rain continued to fall, dampening his shirt and glistening on her cheeks as he tried to decide how to explain. The memory of the night they'd spent together had been with him daily, coiling his gut with sweet, hot desire. He'd never been bothered by such a distraction before and it had irritated him to be robbed of the complete absorption in his work that he'd always taken for granted.

So he'd fought to regain it, plunging into that problem in Saudi, moving on immediately to handle a communication breakdown in Seoul, refusing to call her until he had this disturbing craving under control. But she'd stayed in his mind until finally he'd focused on finishing up as quickly as possible, grimly determined to get back to see her, to settle his unruly emotions. Only to discover his desire for her burned hotter than ever.

Staring down into her face, a feeling of possessiveness swept over him—too strong to be denied, yet too new to be explainable. He abandoned the attempt for the moment, replying instead to the unspoken accusation in her voice. "There haven't been that many women in the past—and the few there were didn't want commitment any more than I did."

"Good for you. Neither do I."

Before he could stop her, she stalked away. Her shoulders were tensed in outrage, her hands fisted at her sides. The slight waddle in her hips made her look like an indignant duck.

He caught up with her at his truck, and she climbed in huffily. Slamming the door behind her, he strode to the other side and turned on the ignition. He didn't try to talk as he drove the narrow, winding road through town, deciding to wait until they got home before continuing the conversation, but he glanced over now and again to where she sat stiffly beside him, staring out the window at the old houses flowing past. His gaze traced the white curve of her cheek, the somber set of her soft mouth.

As if sensing his stare, she looked at him fleetingly, her lips tightening before she turned away. Her light, sweet scent—so hauntingly familiar—drifted his way. Del stared straight ahead again, his hands tightening on the wheel as desire gripped him. He had the urge to park the truck and haul Libby into his arms, to kiss her like he'd thought of kissing her all the time he'd been gone. He'd do it, too, if she hadn't been so angry. Why was she so reluctant to admit the baby was his? Maybe she was worried, wondering how he'd react. It must have been hard on her all these months, handling everything alone.

He frowned at the thought. Surely she knew that now that he was here, he'd take care of everything?

Dusk was falling, lengthening the shadows from the huge trees growing densely in the neighborhood, as he pulled up before the house. The gentle rain continued to drizzle down as, still without speaking, they left the truck to climb the brick walkway to the door and entered the foyer.

When Libby immediately headed toward the stairs, however, he put out a hand to stop her. "We still need to talk about this, Libby." He steered her into what had once been the parlor but was now a den. Inside the room, Libby immediately picked up a blue bundle from an oak side table and sat down calmly on one of the old leather wingback chairs by the fireplace.

Del watched her, momentarily distracted by the blue

snarl of yarn she industriously began poking knitting needles into. "What's that?" he asked curiously.

"Booties."

"I didn't know you could knit," he said in surprise.

"There's a lot," she said repressively, "that you don't know about me."

Del's jaw tightened. Hardly an auspicious start to the conversation, he thought. She didn't look up, the silver needles clicking in uneven but determined rhythm. He could feel his temper rising and fought to hold it down. "There's one thing I *do* know," he said, his tone harsher than he'd intended. "That's *my* baby you're carrying."

"You can't be sure of that."

Despite his resolve not to get angry, his voice roughened as he said, "Of course I'm sure. You're not the type of woman to jump directly from my bed into another man's. Hell, even if you were, there's no way you'd get away with it in Lone Oak, not with Christine in the house and our nosy neighbor living next door."

"No one saw *you*," she reminded him.

"That was sheer luck. How often is the town shut down by a blizzard? Probably once every fifty years. If I hadn't arrived so late at night like I did, and left so early the day the snow finally stopped, *someone* would have seen me. I'm just surprised Mrs. Peyton wasn't waiting at the window with binoculars when we shoveled out the truck."

"She did notice the driveway had been cleared," Libby admitted. "I told her I'd done it alone."

"Exactly my point," Del said triumphantly. "Nothing gets by that lady."

Concentrating on a snag in the blue yarn, Libby said

slowly, "Okay, so maybe there hasn't been anyone since you left. But who's to say I wasn't with another man before I came to Lone Oak—before I met you?"

"You weren't."

The wariness in her expression deepened. "How do you know?"

He stared at her in exasperation. "I know because if you'd made love with someone before you came to Lone Oak, then you wouldn't have been a virgin when you made love with *me*."

"Oh," she said flatly. "You noticed that."

"Of course I noticed that! Do you think I'm an idiot?" She opened her mouth to reply and he pointed a warning finger in her direction. "Don't you *dare* answer that."

She shut her mouth again and bent back over her needles. Slightly mollified, he paused, studying her downcast face. A tinge of pink had crept up under her pale skin and she steadfastly refused to meet his gaze. She was embarrassed, he realized suddenly. She wasn't used to sleeping with men—or talking about it, either. More of his anger melted. Taking a deep breath he said quietly, "Libby…you had to know I realized it was your first time."

The flush deepened in her cheeks. "How should I? You never said anything."

"Neither did you—and I hardly had a chance, did I? The phone rang before we were awake and I had to leave within the hour. But I told you I'd be back…that we'd talk then. Damn it, is that what this is all about?" His voice softened and he stepped forward, tugging her up into his arms. Ignoring the resistance in her stiff figure and the bulge of baby between them, he put his arms around her. Pressing her face into his shirt, he murmured into her sweet-smelling hair, "I'm sorry. I should have called. I just got caught up in—"

He broke off, wondering how to explain, and she lifted her head. "More *important* things?" she said sweetly.

"More *urgent* things," he corrected, pressing her face against him again. "I was trying to finish up as quickly as possible to get back so we could..."

"Take up where we left off?" she said in a muffled voice.

"Talk," he said grimly. Taking her by the shoulders, he held her away, giving her a small shake. "Stop putting words in my mouth and admit this baby's mine."

She remained still in his grasp, searching his face. Then her lashes swept down, hiding her expression as she admitted reluctantly, "You're the father."

An intense wave of satisfaction washed over Del, catching him by surprise. He knew it! He *knew* she hadn't slept with any other man. His hold on her tightened, and he said encouragingly, "See, that wasn't so hard, was it?"

She didn't respond, and Del gave her another hug. Beneath his palms he could feel the delicate bones of her back. Her breasts were crushed softly against his chest, the harder press of her belly nudged his groin. She felt so slight, so vulnerable, in his hold. She'd been through so much without anyone to lean on. But that was all over now; she had nothing to worry about any longer. Possessive tenderness poured through him and words he'd never intended to say sprang out of his mouth, "I'll marry you."

He clamped his lips shut. But after a brief moment of shock he found to his amazement the words felt right. Marriage—he'd never thought it would be a viable option with his type of job, but now...yeah, that was the answer to the problem. The easiest solution.

She wouldn't be on his mind so much if he was married to her.

Libby hadn't responded—overcome with gratitude, no doubt. Pleased that he'd solved everything so easily, he gave her another hug. "It shouldn't be too bad," he said, thinking aloud. "We can just go on in pretty much the same way we've started." Warming to the idea, he added, "In fact, it might be kind of nice to have a wife to come home to in between jobs. I'll tell everyone that I'm the father and—"

"No!" Libby pushed free of his arms.

Her hair was all ruffled, her brown eyes snapping. Del stared at her angry expression in surprise. "You mean you want to be the one to tell everyone?"

"No! I mean I don't want anyone to know you're the father. Not ever."

4

She was overly tired or feverish, Del decided, noting the bright spots of color on her cheeks. Or possibly her raging hormones were confusing her. Soothingly, he said, "Libby, you're not making sense. People are bound to know I'm the father when we get married—"

"We're not getting married."

Seeing the set expression on her face, his noble feeling of self-sacrifice faded. Frowning, he said pointedly, "But we *have* to get married. *You're having my baby!*"

"You know that, and I know that, but nobody else does," Libby remarked, stepping away from him to resume her seat. She picked up her yarn again. "And that's the beauty of *my* plan."

"What plan?"

"To keep you entirely out of this. After all, it wasn't your fault I got pregnant."

He raked his hand through his hair, barely resisting the urge to clutch at it. "But we just established it *was* my fault."

"No, we didn't. We merely established that you're the father," she said, working her needles. "We used a condom. How were you to know I'd get pregnant?"

"No one could know that."

"That's where you're wrong. I did know—or at least I should have." Libby paused in her knitting and looked up at Del. He was standing in the middle of the room, his expression a mixture of bafflement and anger. Choosing her words carefully to help him understand, she said, "Don't you see? This baby is the story of my life. Whenever I do something wrong, I get caught."

His mouth thinned in exasperation. "That's ridiculous."

Libby shook her head. "No, it isn't. My mother's wild—really wild—but no matter what she does, how outrageously she acts, she never has to suffer the consequences. I, on the other hand, always do."

Realizing from his skeptical expression he still didn't believe her, Libby elaborated. "At seven I stole a gum ball—one little pink gum ball from the corner grocery store when I was visiting my dad—and I got caught. My dad was so angry he sent me back to my mom early. At thirteen, a girl handed me her cigarette to hold in the school rest room and that's when the principal marched in. I was suspended and sent to another school. In college, I went skinny-dipping in the college pool with a bunch of girlfriends one Saturday night, and I was the only one caught totally nude by the local police. Is it any wonder I stayed a virgin until I was twenty-six?"

She sighed, picking absently at a fuzzy ball on the yarn. "That, and the fact that the men I met were usually simply interested in meeting my famous mother. But with you, I felt…special. Hah! So much for trying to be 'wild and free,'" she said bitterly.

Del eyed her intently. "Is that what our making love was to you? A chance to be wild and free?"

She nodded. "Instead, I made the biggest mistake of my life."

About to reach for her again, he paused, his brows lowering over his eyes. "You think this baby is the biggest mistake of your life?"

"Not the baby," she admitted. He relaxed a little, only to stiffen as she added, "You. *You're* the mistake."

Scowling, Del put his hands on his hips. "What's wrong with me?"

"Well, to begin with, you're exactly the sort of man my mother always gets involved with."

Del had no idea what type of man Libby's mother liked, but instinctively he knew he didn't appreciate the comparison. "I am not," he denied.

"Yes, you are," Libby answered, primly folding her hands on the bulge of her stomach. "To begin with, you don't want to get married. I don't know how many times I've heard Christine mention it and you certainly made it clear enough before we…got involved. You said your type of job makes marriage an impossibility."

"It does—for a real marriage. For goodness' sake, I'm out of the country ten months out of the year. But we don't have a choice. You're pregnant and I'm willing to live up to my responsibilities by marrying you."

"Thank you, but no thank you," Libby said grimacing. "I've made one mistake—I certainly don't intend to make another. I would never marry a man simply because he feels obligated. In fact, you're not the kind of man I want to marry at all."

"Why not?" Del demanded, his scowl deepening.

Libby held up her hand to count off on her fingers. "You're the kind of man who prefers an affair to marriage. The kind of man who is never around. You'd be a poor risk as a husband, and you certainly don't seem like father material. I want a man who is steady, family minded and dependable. A man who has an eight-to-five job and comes home every night."

"And just where do you think you'll find this paragon?"

"I don't know. Maybe in Lone Oak," she said, disregarding his sarcastic tone. "Which is why I want to keep your identity as the baby's father a secret. People have accepted me here…and I like that," she admitted gruffly, smoothing down a wrinkle in her jumper. "If they know I slept with you—after only knowing you a couple of days!—their opinion of me is bound to change."

"They'd understand—"

"No, they wouldn't. And I refuse to take that chance."

He scowled. "Are you saying you no longer want a physical relationship with me?"

She took a deep breath. "I'm saying I don't want any kind of a relationship with you at all."

For some reason, that statement stunned Del more than learning about the baby. His angry surprise must have shown in his face because her eyes widened and he quickly reined in the revealing emotion, forcing his expression to go blank. She had the right, after all, to terminate their physical relationship. They'd made no promises, exchanged no vows. But still her attitude bothered him. The baby aside, hadn't she felt the same hungry yearning for him all these months that he'd felt for *her?*

Apparently not.

He tried again. "Don't you want the baby to know her real father?"

She thought about that a moment. "If during your brief visits to Lone Oak you want to be involved in *his* life, I'm sure we can come to some reasonable arrangement," she decided magnanimously. "We'll wait and see how things go."

"And if I refuse to hide the fact that the baby is mine?" he asked.

"Then I'll move somewhere else and start over."

Del met her steady brown eyes. She'd do it, too. That determined expression was on her face again. He sighed in exasperation. Any other woman—any normal woman—would be making demands. But not Libby. How could he have forgotten how independent, how *stubborn*, she could be? He remembered the morning after they'd made love. When he received that phone call from work, Libby had been out of bed and dressed before he was, stubbornly insisting she'd help him shovel out his truck. Nothing he'd said could deter her, and finally he'd quit trying, touched by her eagerness to help.

Now, he wondered if maybe she simply hadn't been anxious to speed him on his way.

"What about medical costs? Insurance?" he asked.

"My father left me a little money. I can handle the medical costs," she said firmly.

He should just let her try, he thought, a muscle twitching in his jaw. He should walk out of her life and take the next plane back to Seoul. After all, he'd come to get Libby off his mind and she was making it easy for him. Why was he arguing when she'd made her feelings all too clear? The passion she'd felt that night—and she *had* felt the full fulfillment of that passion, he had no doubts on that score—was obviously no longer important.

All she cared about was the baby.

Well, he cared about the baby, too. He frowned. Sort of. Despite that kick against his hand, the baby was rather a nebulous concept—not quite real. Unlike Libby, with her hollowed-out cheeks and tired eyes.

His frown darkened. He couldn't let her carry this burden alone, no matter how much she claimed to want him to. His conscience wouldn't allow him to abdicate his moral responsibility in the situation—or ignore the drawn expression on Libby's face. She might think she could handle everything herself, but anyone seeing those circles under her eyes had to know better. Independence was fine, but not when a woman was more than seven months' pregnant. Unless she was careful, Libby was going to ruin her own health and that of the baby's.

His resolve hardened. He wouldn't let that happen. She'd never lived on her own before; she probably was underestimating how much the baby would cost. He'd make her see things his way. But not tonight. All this arguing couldn't be good for her, and besides, he had time to change her mind before he left. She just needed a chance to realize marriage was the most practical solution.

"Fine," he said abruptly. "We won't tell anyone that I'm the father, at least until I see how things go."

Libby stared at him with wide eyes. "What are you talking about?"

"I'm going to stick around a couple more days to make sure you're handling everything as well as you think you are." He frowned, eyeing her consideringly. "You look tired to me."

Libby stiffened. Setting aside her knitting, she rose to her feet as quickly as her protruding tummy would allow. "That's not necessary, Del. You don't need to stay," she protested, her voice rising. "I'm doing fine—everything's fine."

"Good. Then it won't matter if I make sure." Ignoring her stuttering protest, he raised his hand for quiet, listening as a car drove up. "That has to be Chris. I'll tell her to park in the garage and we'll unload in the morning. You need to get to bed."

"Wait! We haven't settled this yet," Libby said on a panicky note.

"Yes, we have, so don't waste any more time arguing," he said, striding to the door. With his hand on the knob, he turned to look back, his blue eyes gleaming. "You might as well face it, Libby. Once again, you've been caught."

5

Even the next morning the memory of Del saying the words—with that mockingly satisfied tone in his voice—had the power to infuriate Libby all over again.

"I have not been caught," she firmly told the small brown teddy bear sitting innocently on the mahogany dresser in her bedroom.

Teddy regarded her blankly with black, shoe-button eyes and Libby admitted, "At least not by him. By the baby, now that's a different story."

Yes, she'd definitely been caught by the baby. The realization continually amazed her. How could she love anyone as intensely as she loved this unknown small person nestled beneath her heart?

When she had first suspected she was pregnant, panic had welled up inside her. Alone in her tiny bathroom, nervously fumbling through the directions on the home pregnancy kit, she'd never felt so scared in her life. She didn't want a child; she was just starting to get her own life on track. She'd been accepted at Southern Oregon State to finish up her master's degree and she'd found a part-time job at the department store to help meet her expenses. Yet when that little indicator stick had turned pink, a tide of joy had lifted inside her, filling her with a deep satisfaction that hadn't changed from that moment on.

No, not morning sickness, financial worries—not even problems with Del—could make her regret this baby.

Reaching out, she idly sifted the soft fur on Teddy's belly through her fingers, admitting, "I may not have started off right, but I plan on being the best mother there ever was. I told Del I'm handling everything just fine, but he won't listen to me."

Her mouth twisted wryly. Which was ironic, now that she thought about it. It was because he had listened so intently, his eyes fastened on her face in the candlelight while she revealed feelings she'd never shared with anyone before, that had made her feel so close to him during that long-ago snowstorm.

What an illusion. You'd think, coming from her mother's house where no one was ever what they appeared to be, that she would have been smarter. And yet she still hadn't learned. Even last night, she'd been in danger of falling for him all over again. How could she have thought, even for one brief second, that there might be something more behind his proposal than obligation? Held tight in his arms, feeling so secure resting against him, she'd almost expected him to say he...cared about her.

She picked up Teddy and gave him a gentle shake. "It's not me he's concerned about—or even the baby. He just wants to placate his conscience before he takes off again. Well, I have no intention of obliging him. I'm completely over him, I tell you. He's nothing more to me than my landlady's brother—"

Libby paused, a soft knock interrupting her. A second later Christine popped her head inside the door, her dark hair tumbling around her mischievous face. "Hello, is this a private conversation or can anyone join in?" She returned Libby's smile before her gaze fell on Teddy. Her blue eyes lit up. "Oh, what a darling! Where did you get him?" she asked, coming closer to admire the small bear.

"Dorrie Jean brought him over yesterday." Libby relinquished the stuffed toy to her friend and sat down on an old wooden rocker in a corner of the room. With a small sigh, she picked up her knitting.

"How sweet of her!" Christine exclaimed. "What did Mrs. P. bring?"

Libby unraveled her yarn—how did it always manage to get so twisted?—and started another laborious line of purling. "More warnings on the terror of childbirth," she said dryly.

Christine hooted. "As if she'd know—Dorrie Jean was adopted." Still smiling, she flopped back on Libby's bed, then turned to prop her chin on her elbow, cuddling the bear next to her.

Libby smiled at her, thinking, as she always did, how much—and how little—Christine was like her brother. Even to the most casual observer, the resemblance between the two was obvious. Both were tanned and long limbed, with dark curls and brilliant blue eyes. But Del clipped his curls short and combed them ruthlessly back, while Christine's hair bounced rebelliously to her shoulders. Del's masculine nose had a slight bump from being broken at some time. Christine's nose was small and straight.

But the biggest difference between the two was their

expressions. Del's was usually guarded, hiding his thoughts, while Christine's was open and friendly, reflecting a lively interest in the people around her.

Christine examined the polish on her long nails, saying, "Mrs. P. means well, you know."

"I know," Libby admitted.

"In fact," Christine added, buffing her nails on her shirt and checking them again, "Del means well, too."

Libby's heart skipped a beat. She looked up, meeting her friend's eyes with a question in her own.

Christine grinned. "I'd have to be an idiot not to notice what an interest he took in you." Her brow puckered. "Although, I've never seen Del act so domineering before. Of course, he always tries to boss me around. I guess because you live in our house, he's treating you like a sister, too."

Breathing a thankful sigh of relief that Christine hadn't guessed the true reason for Del's behavior, Libby resumed her knitting, saying, "There's no reason for him to feel that way."

"I know, but you'll never convince him of that. Del's a real take-charge kind of guy. Which isn't all bad," Chris added fairly. "When Dad died, Del was only sixteen, but he stepped right into the role of man of the house." She winced. "And believe me, with a house this old and big, that was quite a job. Something always needed fixing—the wiring, the plumbing—and money, of course, was pretty tight. It became even more of a struggle when Mom died a few years later. It wasn't until Del finished up college and found a job with Visatek that things started loosening up again. He really loves that computer stuff."

Libby had seen the computer Del used while at

home. The machine, stolid and imposing, dominated a corner of the study. She paused in her knitting. "Do you think he'll stay long?"

"Probably no more than a day or two. The jobs he handles are usually pretty much a one-man operation."

Libby regarded her friend with a slight frown. "What exactly does he do for a living, Chris," she asked slowly. "You've never really said." And neither had he.

"Haven't I?" Christine looked surprised. "I guess I assumed you knew. He's an electronic engineer specializing in reconnaissance systems—if that tells you anything. His background is in computer imagery, information systems—" she made a face "—boring stuff, like that. Thank goodness he can't talk about it. The projects he works on are code 'black'—which means even the titles are hush-hush."

"I see." Libby rocked a minute, mulling that over. It sounded like such a lonely life, and yet... "He must enjoy it," she said, thinking aloud.

"He's enjoys the challenge—and he's good at it," Chris replied. "Not only at data analysis, but at the technical stuff, too. He can fix just about anything. There were a ton of companies that wanted him and with whom he wouldn't have had to do so much traveling, but Visatek offered too much to resist. He insisted on putting me through college, you know. I got out as quickly as I could."

Libby knew Christine had finished four years of college in three, then jumped right into her job as a buyer. Libby, on the other hand, had spent more than eight years trying to reach her goal of a master's degree and a teaching credential and still hadn't succeeded. She had at least another semester to complete. "You're lucky to be doing what you want to do," Libby said.

Chris smiled ruefully. "Del said a degree would help me get the job—and he was right. Mom, too, had always wanted me to get at least a bachelor's degree. She said a college education was an investment in the future."

Libby tried to imagine Liz giving such practical advice. She couldn't. Her mother lived in such a dreamworld—plunging into each new role with wholehearted fervor, riding on a never-ending emotional roller coaster—that Libby had finally realized she'd have to get away if she ever planned to have a real, "normal" life of her own.

It hadn't been easy to leave. Especially since in the past few years Liz had begun to rely on her as something of an unpaid "social secretary," always available to handle whatever "crisis" should arise—and crises were always occurring around Liz, who thrived on the drama of emotional chaos.

But Libby didn't. And eight months ago, when once again a manufactured "emergency" of her mother's forced Libby to drop another class in order to find time to deal with the problem, she'd packed up and left immediately afterward, ignoring her mother's tirade about her daughter's "selfishness."

Libby had transferred her credits to Southern Oregon State University, choosing the college for two reasons: First, because it was close enough to get home quickly if Liz should ever *really* need her; and second, because the campus was close to Lone Oak, the small town Libby had once driven through on a trip with her father and had never forgotten.

Her knitting dropped into her lap and she rocked a couple of moments, staring unseeingly out the window. Yet, once again, in spite of her efforts, she'd gotten offtrack. "Maybe I can finish up my degree when the baby is born..."

"Plenty of time to worry about that later," Christine said, a comforting refrain she'd used often during the past several months whenever Libby fretted about the future. Chris fiddled with one of Teddy's stubby arms as she gave a considering glance around the small room. "One thing you should do before the baby comes, though, is to move to a room downstairs—or at least to the second floor. Del said he thought you looked worn-out, and the climb all the way up here has to be hard on you. There's a large bedroom next to his that's nice..."

"I'm fine up here," Libby said firmly. So she looked worn-out to him, did she? How flattering. Well, she had no intention of moving closer to Del—or his bedroom with all its memories of that night. "I'm not tired at all," she added for good measure.

Christine gave her a skeptical glance and Libby amended the statement, saying, "Okay, maybe I am a little bit but that's normal for a woman in my condition. Besides, I love it up here," she added truthfully.

The third floor—her "flat" she considered it—had been the maid's quarters once upon a time. Smaller than the first two floors, it consisted of three cramped rooms tucked under a sloping ceiling, a closet-sized bathroom and a narrow angled passageway. The room they were now in was the smallest of the three, but feminine and bright. The ceiling pressed down, but a west-facing dormer window boxed in the afternoon sun, while even on the cloudiest of days the morning light flooded in through the two knee-high windows opposite to dance among the tiny pink roses scattered on the cream-colored wallpaper. "I'm going to paint the little room next door blue for the baby and use the back room for a sitting room," Libby told her friend.

Chris smiled. "Sounds great. If you need more furniture, check the loft in the garage. I think there's a bassinet up there."

"Thanks." Libby looked fondly at the worn antiques around her—a tarnished brass bed, a mahogany dressing table with a clouded mirror, the broad rocking chair in which she was sitting. She loved the aura of timelessness surrounding the old furniture. Her mother's taste had run to brash, modern pieces that looked "artistic" but never felt comfortable when you sat in them.

Rocking absently, she gazed out the window at the oak leaves fluttering in the light morning breeze. The thought of the way the building had sheltered family after family charmed her. "This is such a wonderful old house," she said softly.

Christine made a face. "You think so? Personally, I'd rather have an apartment in a big city where there's a chance of some excitement—and I will as soon as I snag another couple of promotions."

"Really?" Libby said in surprise. "You'd prefer an apartment to this?"

Chris nodded. "Yep, give me a modern, low-care condo any day." She wrinkled her small nose. "No matter what you do, old houses always smell like musty books and lemon polish. I think Del feels the same but this house has been in our family for generations, so he's hesitated to—omigosh!''

She bolted up so suddenly that Libby squeaked in alarm, drawing her feet up beneath her off the wooden floor. "What is it! A mouse?"

Chris looked at her in surprise and then laughed merrily. "Good gracious, no. I just remembered Del's waiting for us in the parlor. He piled all your presents in there."

Bouncing to her feet, Christine headed for the door carrying Teddy with her, only to pause as a thought struck her. She looked back at Libby, who hadn't moved from the rocker. "Why, have you seen a mouse lately?" she demanded.

Libby nodded reluctantly. Chris declared, "I'd better tell Del," and bounded down the stairs before Libby could protest that she didn't mind a little mouse running around. Well, she did, but she certainly didn't want Del to kill it.

"Libby!" Christine called from the stairwell. "Are you coming?"

"Be right there."

Setting her knitting aside, Libby forced herself to get up and went to the dressing table. Picking up her brush she ran it through her hair. She wasn't anxious to see Del again. Already her stomach was twisting and turning and for once it wasn't because of the baby's antics. Thank goodness he was only staying a day or two. She didn't have the energy for any more.

She leaned forward, eyeing herself in the foggy glass. She did look a little peaked; she'd have to ask the doctor for a stronger iron pill or something. But for now... She picked up some cover-up and daubed the makeup on the mauve circles beneath her eyes. There! Surely Del wouldn't notice them now.

Del noticed as soon as she came in the parlor. He glanced away, pretending to examine a couple of gift boxes to hide his frown. He'd hoped a good night's sleep would erase her air of fragility, but obviously it hadn't done the trick. Libby moved slowly, without energy, settling into an armchair with an unconscious sigh.

His lips straightened into a firm line. No doubt about it—he needed to accompany her to the doctor and find out if her tiredness was normal or not. She wouldn't like his decision, he knew, so he didn't comment on his plans, saying instead, "Chris says you saw a mouse."

"Only a small one," Libby replied, as if the size of the rodent made a difference. "And just a few times."

"Or maybe you've seen several different mice one time each," he countered dryly. "I'll set some traps."

Ignoring the small sound of protest Libby made, he turned to his sister. "Better give me a list of everything else that needs to be done around this place and I'll get on it while I'm here. I know the gutters need cleaning, and the batteries changed in the smoke detectors—"

"I just did that," Libby said.

Both Delaneys turned to look at her. Christine looked startled, while Del's brows drew over his eyes in a frown. "You changed the batteries in the smoke detectors?" he asked.

Libby nodded. "And I cleaned out the gutters, too.

I noticed during the last rainstorm that they were getting clogged with leaves. You can see them from my room.''

Christine's eyes widened and Del's voice grew dangerously quiet as he demanded, ''Are you telling me you climbed a thirty-foot ladder to clear the gutters?''

''Of course not. I climbed out on the roof through my window and just swept them out.'' Slightly perplexed at their reaction, she added, ''It's just something I used to do when I stayed at my father's as a kid. I didn't think you'd mind.''

''Mind! Of course we don't mind!'' Christine exclaimed while Del stood there with his mouth pressed in a tight line. ''It's just that it's so dangerous in your condition. You have to be more careful, Libby.''

''Damn right she has to be more careful,'' Del said. ''If that isn't the—''

''You know he's right, Lib,'' Chris interrupted. ''What if something happened to the baby?''

Prepared to expand—in detail—on this point, Del was blocked as Chris added hastily, ''Anyway, let's not talk anymore about it. There are presents to open.'' She put one in Libby's lap saying, ''This one's from Brooke.''

Still smoldering with anger that Libby had taken such a risk, Del watched from across the room as she accepted the gift, her face filling with such unconscious anticipation that his temper cooled in reluctant enjoyment of her pleasure.

Her brown eyes softened as she carefully unwrapped a box to reveal tiny blue jeans and a diminutive shirt. ''How darling,'' she breathed. Her lips curved gently upward and Del realized suddenly it was the first he'd seen her smile since his return. She certainly hadn't smiled at *him*.

But this morning the expression came readily, lighting her face with subdued excitement as Christine handed her gift after gift. Soon a pile of miniature pastel garments grew beside her chair. Her slim fingers traced the delicate embroidery on the little outfits, stroking the soft terry and brushed flannel from which they were made. Del's eyes half shut in remembered pleasure. She'd touched him with that same hesitant enjoyment the night they'd made love.

When she opened Christine's gift, Libby's mouth formed a soundless "O." "It's beautiful," she breathed, lifting from the box a pure white blanket, knitted in soft angora yarn. She held it against her cheek, and Del thought the blanket looked no softer than her creamy skin as she gazed mistily up at Christine. "You made it, didn't you?" she said. "Oh, how I wish I could knit as well as you."

"You'll get there," Chris said, bending down to give her a quick, impulsive hug. "I've had years of practice, growing up in a small town where there's not much to do. You'll be churning out all kinds of blankets in no time."

Libby carefully folded the blanket and returned it to the box, saying ruefully, "I can't even finish one booty."

"Even if you don't, it doesn't look like the kid will miss it," Del pointed out, eying all the baby items scattered around the room.

"Are you kidding?" Christine exclaimed, wadding up an armful of tissue paper. "This isn't half the stuff she'll need. Susan says her kids went through three or four outfits a day."

Del was dumbstruck. "For one little kid?"

Chris nodded. "And she still needs a swing, a high chair, a crib, a car seat— Oh, wait—that carrier Brooke gave you doubles as a car seat for the first few months, doesn't it? Which reminds me—" she turned to her brother "—don't forget to gas up the truck before you drive Libby to the doctor's. It's running on empty."

"So what else is new?" he asked, pretending not to notice the small start Libby gave at Christine's statement. He continued thumbing through the baby book he was holding, saying to his sister, "I've told you time and time again that you're going to burn out the engine if you keep trying to run on fumes."

Christine made a face. "Nag, nag, nag. Oh, don't glare at me. You've made your point. I'm sorry, and to prove it I'll make breakfast—or would it be considered brunch now? Anyway, prepare yourselves for a culinary delight of scrambled eggs and toast."

"Mushy eggs and burnt bread, more likely," Del said dryly as she strode out of the room. He glanced over at Libby, adding wryly, "She sounds like she's doing us a favor but she's probably trying to avoid helping pick up. That sister of mine is a spoiled one."

Libby smiled perfunctorily, but brought up the subject that concerned her more. "Del..." she said, slowly. "What did Chris mean about you driving me to the doctor's?"

He glanced up, his eyes narrowing slightly as he prepared for another argument. "She meant exactly that. I told her I'd take you since I had to go into Vicksville, anyway.''

"I can drive myself—"

"Christine said you've been having dizzy spells."

She bit her lip. "Christine certainly talks a lot."

He nodded. "She sure does, but maybe in this instance that's a good thing. Do you think it's wise to try and drive in your condition?''

Libby didn't, but she didn't want him to drive her, either. "But my visit isn't for a couple of days," she protested.

He shrugged. "I told you I can manage the time off." He picked up a mint green T-shirt and eyed it dubiously. "Are these things big enough?''

"Of course they are. That's a size one. Newborn sizes are even smaller. As I was saying last night, there's no need for you to stay—''

"And I said there was."

Libby clenched her hands on top of the box in her lap, holding on to her temper. "But I thought you were in the middle of an important project. Aren't you worried they'll replace you?''

"No," he answered absently, still busy picking through the pile of gifts next to her chair. "When you've put in as much time as I have and covered as many positions on the way up, there aren't too many people they can replace you with—not too quickly, anyway. Besides, I can handle the preliminaries from here. What the hell is this?" He lifted a clear plastic tube, which contained another inside.

Libby could feel a blush rising in her cheeks. "Nothing."

He must have caught the constricted note in her

voice because he glanced at her curiously, then looked back down at the object in his hands. "Obviously it's something or why would someone have given it to you?" He pulled on the inner tube, sliding it back and forth in the outer. The movement caused a slight sucking sound. "Is it a—?"

"It's a breast pump, for goodness' sake. Will you just give it to me?" Libby reached up and snatched it out of his hands, her fury growing as she noticed the grin on his face. "These aren't all toys, you know. Having a baby is serious."

His smile disappeared. "I know it is—which reminds me of something I've been meaning to talk to you about." He leveled an accusing stare at her. "What's the real reason you didn't get that ultrasound Mrs. P. was talking about? And don't bother giving me that cock-and-bull story you told her about you and the doctor changing your minds. I could tell you weren't telling the truth."

"Yes, I was."

He stared at her steadily. Silence filled the room. Libby couldn't quite hold his gaze. "Ultrasounds are pretty expensive," she admitted.

His mouth thinned in exasperation, and she added hastily, "It's not a necessary procedure in my case anyway, Del, just precautionary. The doctor wasn't concerned when I decided to pass on it."

"Well, I'm concerned, which is precisely why I'm going with you to see that doctor and find out for myself what's going on."

She huffed in exasperation. "And once you find out, you'll leave me alone? Go back to your job?"

"Of course I will."

"Then fine. You can come with me."

"Good."

Libby breathed a sigh of relief that turned into a groan as he slowly added, "Just one more thing..."

"What now?" she almost wailed.

"I think we should let the doctor know I'm the father."

Libby tensed in alarm. "No! I told you last night I don't want anyone to know."

"It's not as if we'll be telling the entire town," he told her patiently. He picked up a yellow rubber duck someone had given her, tossing the squeaky toy from one hand to the other as he added, "But I think the doctor should know. Think about it, Libby," he interrupted when she would have argued further. "What if something happens to you—or the baby. What if she—"

"*He!*"

"Needs blood or other medical help that only you or I—as the mother or father—can give? I need to be on record somewhere so I can be contacted. Have you thought about any of that?"

"Of course I have—I just..." She broke off. She'd just put it out of her mind. The endless possibilities had worried her so much she hadn't known what else to do.

But everything he'd said was all too true. She had to let him be involved—at least this much. The baby's life might depend on it.

She looked up. Del was watching her intently. Meeting her gaze, he said quietly, "You know I'm right. We have to tell the doctor. For the baby's sake."

Who could argue against that? "Okay," she said reluctantly. "For the baby's sake."

6

Del shifted in his chair a few days later, glancing around at the doctor's waiting room where he and Libby had been sitting for the past half hour. The walls were painted a bright yellow and decorated with huge animals—orange giraffes, blue lions, plump pink elephants—all lined up to enter a stout brown boat. Probably some kind of surreal Noah's ark thing, he decided.

He shifted again, trying to find enough room between a miniature child's table and chair set up in the middle of the small room to stretch his legs. He felt uncomfortable; not because he was the only man in the room because he wasn't—the other woman waiting was accompanied by her husband—nor even because the pink elephants on the wall looked like a Pepto-Bismol nightmare. No, the major reason he felt a little awkward was because of Libby's persistent coolness.

Del slanted a glance at her aloof profile. She'd braided her hair today in two long pigtails that made her look more like seventeen than twenty-six. Pink ribbons, the same color as the blouse she wore—and the elephants on the wall—were tied at the ends. One of the bows had come untied. Without thinking, Del lifted a hand to fix it and she reached up and flipped the braid over her shoulder, not even sparing him a glance.

Del grimaced. No doubt about it, she was making it abundantly clear that while she might have given in to his desire to accompany her, she certainly wasn't pleased with him. She'd avoided him as much as possible the past two days and had barely said a word on the entire forty-minute trip to the doctor's. Now she continued to ignore him, her gaze fixed steadily on the parenting magazine in her hands.

His lips tightened and he crossed his arms over his chest. He wasn't used to Libby being so quiet. She hadn't been a chatterer during the snowstorm but she had talked to him—quite a bit, in fact. About growing up with her famous mother, Liz; about Nicholas, the father she'd rarely seen. She'd shared her thoughts on life—even her misguided views on politics. He'd enjoyed listening to her, teasing her, watching her sweetly serious expression or the sudden laughter that would light her face at his occasional wry comment.

He wasn't much of a conversationalist himself. Being unable to talk about his job for some reason made him more reticent about other things, as well. But with Libby, that hadn't been a problem. She'd been fascinated by his stories about his family and how it had been growing up in a small town. Conversation between them had just flowed.

Del scowled. Hell, they hadn't only been lovers during that snowstorm, they'd also become friends. He wanted to restore at least a little of the rapport they'd had on his last visit and this was one of the only opportunities he'd had to be alone with her without Christine hovering about somewhere.

Libby put down the magazine and he looked up hopefully. Without a word she stepped over his legs and headed into the rest room.

Del heaved a long-suffering sigh.

The man sitting across from him must have heard it. Pushing his glasses higher on his nose, he leaned closer, asking, "This your first?"

Del looked at him, then nodded.

"Ours, too," the man said and thrust out a hand. "I'm Ken. Ken Patterson."

Del accepted the proffered handshake as Ken indicated the blonde sitting demurely beside him. She nodded graciously at Del as her husband added dramatically, "And this is Barbie."

Ken beamed expectantly. Del regarded him blankly, and the other man's smile faded. "Don't you get it? Ken and Barbie. You know. Like the dolls?"

"Oh, yeah. Cute," Del said and then stared at the bathroom door. What the hell was taking Libby so long? Was she sick?

Ken started talking again, interrupting his train of thought. "Our baby is due in October." Both Pattersons glowed with pride, as if, Del thought, they were the only ones who'd ever had a baby.

Barbie added, "So when is your wife due, Mr....?"

"Delaney. Del Delaney," he answered automatically, then paused. Strangely reluctant to admit Libby wasn't his wife, Del compromised, saying, "Libby's not due for another six weeks."

Ken's face sharpened with interest. "Hey, we'll

probably be in the same childbirth class. You have signed up, haven't you?''

Had Libby signed up? "I'm not sure," Del admitted. Ken looked surprised and Barbie's perfectly plucked eyebrows rose. Del added a little defensively, "I just got back in town. I've been out of the country.''

The other man's expression cleared and Barbie leaned forward, saying graciously, "I'm sure your wife is thankful to have you back.''

Not hardly, Del thought.

"What are you having?" Barbie asked. "A boy or a girl?''

"A girl," Del said decisively.

"Oh. We're having a boy," Barbie said, the faintly superior note in her voice annoying Del no end. "We decided to have a boy first, and then maybe a little girl.''

Something in her tone made it sound as if having a girl first was entirely the wrong decision—as if *their* boy was somehow superior to *his* girl. Del stifled a snort. As if any child these two could produce would even come near to the superior offspring Libby was carrying.

He picked up a magazine, pretending to be engrossed in the article "Breast or Bottle: How to Decide" so that the Pattersons would leave him alone. The ruse worked...until Libby returned. No sooner had she sat down again than Barbie leaned forward to say commiseratingly, "It gets pretty tiring, doesn't it? Running to the rest room all the time.''

"It sure does," Libby agreed.

Encouraged by this response, Barbie added, "Your

husband was just telling us your baby is due in October, too.''

''He's not my husband,'' Libby replied promptly—to Del's vast annoyance. ''This is my landlady's brother. He just gave me a ride here.''

Del grimaced behind his magazine. Not only had she jumped to correct the ''husband'' mistake, she couldn't even define him as a friend. ''My landlady's brother.'' He sounded like some kind of second-rate taxi service, for God's sake.

He lowered the magazine to glare at Libby and encountered the Pattersons' stunned looks instead. Both were regarding him as if he'd falsely posed as the President of the United States or something. Disgusted with them—and even more with Libby—he retired back into his magazine as Barbie asked Libby which doctor she had.

''Dr. Cindy Kanuse.''

Over the top edge of his magazine, Del could see Ken and Barbie exchange another glance. Barbie's tone took on an even greater superiority as she stated, ''I have Dr. Daniel Mitchell.'' She giggled. The falsely coy sound made Del grit his teeth, as she elbowed her spouse. ''Ken wasn't too happy about that at first. Not only is Dr. Dan handsome, but he's single. But I told Ken he's the best.''

''And I want you to have the best,'' Ken replied, patting her hand.

''I've met Dr. Dan. He seems very nice,'' Libby said.

Nice, hmm? Del's interest sharpened. Was this the doctor Christine had said was hanging around Libby?

If the guy wasn't her doctor, why was he so interested in her?

His eyes narrowing, he was pondering the probable answer to the question when the nurse called Libby's name. She stood and Del caught her wrist lightly to stop her before she left the room. "Don't forget. I'll be waiting to come in."

Her lips tightened. Nodding curtly, she left.

Wide-eyed again, the Pattersons must have decided he was a depraved impostor. They made no more attempts at conversation. Del finished his article in peace, then turned to another about the treatment for sensitive nipples. After finishing that one, though, he put the magazine down, too keyed up to read. What on earth was the holdup? When they'd checked in, the nurse had said he'd be called in after the initial exam. None of the other women had been gone so long. Had they found something wrong with the baby? With Libby?

He shifted restlessly, then finally gave in to the compulsion to pace. After ten minutes of this fruitless exercise, he reached another decision and leaned into the receptionist's window. The nurse inside glanced up. Aware of Ken and Barbie's interest, Del lowered his voice, saying, "Excuse me, but my...fiancée wanted me to join her so I could ask the doctor some questions."

The receptionist nodded. "Perhaps they've forgotten. Let me check."

Ken and Barbie goggled at him, but Del ignored them, following the nurse uninvited. Reaching the door, she knocked briefly, then poked her head in to say, "Miss Sinclair's fiancé wanted to ask you a couple of questions, Doctor."

"Send him in," Del heard the doctor reply.

The nurse stepped back, almost bumping into Del. She looked surprised to find him there, but smiled and stepped aside so he could enter.

Del walked in. Libby was lying on the examining table, an astonished look on her face. They'd put one of those flimsy hospital gowns on her, and draped a sheet across her lap. The gown gaped open a little, and Del caught a glimpse of the white curve of her belly before she yanked the garment closed and clutched it across the front, anger gathering on her face. Before she could protest his intrusion, Del said quickly to the doctor, "Hello, I'm Del Delaney—the baby's father. I wanted to find out how Libby's doing."

The doctor—a small, attractive brunette in her midthirties with the figure of an eighteen-year-old—swiveled around on the stool upon which she was sitting and gave him a brisk smile. "Glad to meet you, Del. We encourage the fathers to be involved in all stages of the pregnancy. Your help will make things much easier on Libby."

Turning around again, she waved a slender hand. "So grab a seat and sit down. I'm just locating the baby's heartbeat."

Del did as instructed, pulling a straight-backed chair from the wall and straddling it. A gentleman would leave at this point, he knew. It didn't take a genius to realize by the horror in Libby's expression and the shooing motions she kept making behind the doctor's back that she didn't want him to stay.

But he wasn't about to budge. He couldn't. Especially when the doctor parted the gown revealing Libby's stomach. It *did* look as if she'd swallowed a ball—a soccer ball, at least. He watched fascinated as the doctor spread lubricant on the lower curve of that round firm mound before pressing gently against it with a stethoscope.

She'd kill him, Libby decided, squirming as much from Del's intent gaze as the cold metal feel of the stethoscope crawling along her skin. He knew—he had to know—that she hadn't planned on him coming in during the physical exam, but rather much later, when Dr. Kanuse was finished. She felt as helpless and exposed as a beached whale.

Strange noises emerged from the amplifier attached to the scope.

"That's her stomach growling," the doctor explained.

"Sounds like a pack of lions quarreling over a piece of meat," was Del's observation.

Libby shut her eyes. Could she be any more embarrassed? The growling grew fiercer as the stethoscope rolled over her lower belly toward her sheet-draped—thank goodness!—bikini line. Libby flinched.

"Did I hurt you?" the doctor asked.

"She's ticklish there," Del said before she could reply.

Libby flushed at the unbidden memory of him drawing a teasing finger across that sensitive spot. *Go away,* she mouthed desperately in his direction, but he wasn't looking at her face. His absorbed stare was fastened on the stethoscope as the doctor patiently searched for the baby's heartbeat. Libby had just decided to repeat the demand aloud when a squishy, rhythmic beating echoed into the room.

"That's it," the doctor said in satisfaction.

Wonder filled Libby's heart as it always did when she heard the baby's heartbeat. Involuntarily, she glanced at Del. For a fleeting moment the same awe she felt was evident in his startled eyes.

She smiled. "My son," she said softly.

At her words, his usual unreadable expression masked his face again. "Daughter," he corrected. Then his brows drew together. "Isn't it rather rapid?"

"Perfectly normal," the doctor said as the baby rolled over and growling sounds filled the room again. Briskly she removed the stethoscope and handed Libby a towelette to wipe off the lubricant. Walking over to the sink, the doctor washed her hands, saying over her shoulder. "Keep taking your vitamins, Libby. Walk every day. Sexual intercourse is fine at this point..."

Del raised a brow. Libby flushed.

"Is your dizziness easing up?" the doctor asked, wiping her hands on a paper towel.

Libby nodded.

"Good. Let me know if you start getting headaches." The doctor picked up her chart and glanced over it. "The baby is doing just great. However, we still need to work on your weight."

"What's wrong with her weight?" Del asked sharply.

The doctor smiled reassuringly. "She's a bit underweight for her third trimester. Nothing much to worry about, but I want her to gain a few more pounds..."

Del glared in Libby's direction, but fearing what he

might say, she pretended not to notice as she carefully wiped off the lubricant. The last thing she wanted was Del to become involved.

"Also," the doctor continued, "I want her to rest more. Studies have found that standing on her feet all day—as Libby does in her job—increases a woman's risk of having a premature baby."

"It sounds as if you think she should quit working," Del said.

The doctor met his gaze. "It wouldn't hurt if she could quit working, but she tells me that isn't possible."

"It *is* possible, if it will help the baby," Del stated unequivocally. "Isn't it, Libby?"

Angry at his assumption, she tossed the towelette into the trash and wrapped the gown more firmly around her. "We'll talk about it later," she said repressively.

The doctor patted her shoulder. "That's a good idea. Talk it over. I'm sure you'll see that your fiancé is right. After all, Libby, you don't want to endanger yourself or the baby."

The doctor left the room. Barely waiting until the door closed after her, Del said, "What's there to discuss? You need to quit working. If you need financial help, I'm willing to provide it."

Libby sat on the edge of the table, one hand clasping the sheet draped across her lap, the other clutching the front of the gown closed. "I don't want to talk about this now."

"Tough. I do."

"I need to get dressed."

"We need to settle this first."

He stood and her heart jumped. He wasn't playing fair. He seemed so big in the small room. He knew she felt vulnerable and helpless without her clothes on, but he didn't care. He wanted this settled—and, as usual, he wanted it settled *his* way.

She lifted her chin, knowing if she didn't stand her ground now, he'd trample all over her. "You can talk all you want, but I'm not discussing anything until I get dressed."

He didn't like that; she could tell by the frustration on his face. But he obviously knew better than to try to argue. With a sound of disgust, he strode out of the room.

Only waiting long enough to make sure he wasn't going to return, Libby climbed down from the table and hastily pulled on her blouse and jumper. She stepped into her shoes and sat down to tie the laces—a feat that grew harder every day due to her increasing girth. How could the doctor think she was underweight? There had to be some mistake. Surely she couldn't get much bigger.

She stepped out into the hall and found Del waiting for her. She didn't protest as he grasped her arm to lead her out of the back rooms, but when they reached the reception area, she pulled up short. "Wait a minute. I need to pay my bill."

"I'll get it."

"No! I'll pay for it myself."

His jaw tightened. "Don't push me on this, Libby. I'm losing patience."

So was she, Libby decided. "Fine. Pay it," she said. Why argue? She'd simply write him a check and make sure Christine deposited it in his account. She flounced out of the doctor's office without waiting for him, anger blinding her so that she almost bumped into the white-coated figure just entering the building.

"Whoa, there!" Strong hands caught her shoulders to steady her, and Libby looked up from the white coat her nose was pressed against to meet Dr. Dan's smiling gaze. "Are you all right?"

"Fine," she said, forcing a smile. "Sorry to almost mow you down like that."

"No problem. I've never been one to object to pretty women running into me," he said with a wink.

Dr. Dan was a handsome man, tall and lean with pleasant gray eyes. Very easy to talk to, Libby had discovered from the few times he'd come into the store where she worked. Right now his teasing grin was wide and white and Libby couldn't resist smiling back. She stepped away and the doctor reluctantly released her, saying, "And why are you in such a hurry to leave, Elizabeth? Do you have to get back to work?"

She shook her head, but before she could explain that Del was with her, Dan asked smoothly, "Then how about lunch? There's a little place down the street—"

"Libby and I were just on our way there," a deep voice said from behind her. Del wrapped a hand around the back of Libby's neck, saying casually, "Would you care to join *us*?"

A growing heat burned in Libby's cheeks as the doctor's gaze rested speculatively on that proprietary hold on her sensitive nape, before returning to scan Libby's face. He said slowly, "Not this time, thanks. Take care, Elizabeth."

With a nod he moved on.

Del stared after him, his eyes narrowing. So that was the wonderful Dr. Dan, was it? He didn't look so wonderful to him. Couldn't Libby see the guy's hair was thinning on top? And just where did the guy get off, flirting with a pregnant woman like that. His hold tightened a little as he glanced down at her. "So are you ready to get something to eat?"

"I'm not hungry." Breaking away from him, she marched toward the parking lot.

Keeping up with her easily, Del caught her arm to steady her as she stumbled on the uneven asphalt, and Libby turned on him, demanding angrily, "What is it with you, acting like that?"

"Like what?" he drawled. She stood without answering, her brown eyes snapping, her hands on her hips. She'd buttoned her blouse crookedly, he noticed, and he reached out to fix it.

Libby slapped his hand away. "Like that! Precisely like that! Like you have the right to tell me what to do—or when to quit work—or even to rebutton my blouse. Despite what you told that nurse in there, you're not really my fiancé, Del, so quit acting like one!"

His brows rose. "Okay, I will—when *you* quit acting like some kind of pregnant superwoman."

"Oh!" She yanked at the truck door handle, forgetting it was locked. Fuming, she waited with tapping foot until Del calmly unlocked it and then she clambered ungracefully up into the seat. "Take me home."

Walking around to the other side, he climbed in and started the engine. "First we'll get something to eat."

She had no intention of accompanying him to the restaurant. "I'm not hungry," she said firmly.

He made a tsking sound with his tongue against his teeth as he pulled into the parking lot. "Don't lie, Libby. I heard your stomach growling in that examining room."

That shut her up long enough for him to usher her into the coffee shop and ensconce her in a booth. Libby hid behind the plastic-coated menu for another few minutes as her cheeks cooled and the old-fashioned atmosphere of the family restaurant exercised a soothing effect.

When the waitress came to take their orders, she managed to say with creditable dignity, "Just a salad, please."

"And chicken soup, too, for the lady," Del tacked on. When the waitress left he met Libby's annoyed look with a bland one. "I've heard chicken soup is good for you."

"If you have a cold," she said haughtily. "I don't think it's going to cure my pregnancy."

"But maybe it will help cure your crankiness," he murmured.

She ignored him as she ate her meal. There was nothing more annoying, she decided twenty minutes later, than a man who was right. She did feel better after eating the rich soup—and much more able to handle the disgustingly satisfied-looking male who sat across from her watching her eat.

Setting down her spoon, she dabbed at her mouth with her napkin and then plunged into the issue at hand. "I can't afford to quit work yet."

"You can't afford not to if you're endangering your health," Del countered, pushing aside his own empty plate. His lips flattened in a straight line as he added, "I have enough money to help tide you over."

Libby met his gaze. "That's beside the point. I told you having this baby was my decision—and my responsibility. I'm going to be a mother. I need to be able to stand on my own two feet."

"And you will, but right now that isn't possible." He added impatiently, "What other choice do you have than to accept my help?"

She picked up her abandoned napkin and absently began shredding it into tiny pieces. Good question. What choice did she have? She didn't have enough money saved up to last until the baby's birth. The inheritance she'd received from her father was a help, but not enough to support her for too long without a job. She'd planned to work at least another month.

"I could call my mother, I suppose..." she said slowly. Liz would help, but she'd take over, too. Leaving her mother's financial stranglehold had been hard enough the first time—it would be well nigh impossible with a small baby. "But she'd have me go back to live with her in California," Libby admitted. She pushed the napkin pieces into a small white pile. "And I don't want to do that."

"Then accept *my* help," Del said firmly. When she didn't answer, he sighed. "C'mon, Libby. Talk to me. Tell me what's wrong."

She added a few more pieces to her napkin mountain. "I just don't want to depend on you—or anyone." She glanced up fleetingly. "I don't want to be...weak."

He looked as if he was about to argue, but she didn't give him the chance, adding fiercely, "Do you know how hard it is to summon ambition when there's always someone there to pick up the bills? Would *you* have worked so hard to get where you are in your job if you hadn't needed to provide for Christine and your mom?''

He frowned. ''Okay—maybe you've got a point. But the situations aren't the same.'' Reaching over, he caught her fidgeting fingers in his big hand. ''I have a moral and financial responsibility to help you—and the baby—that can't be ignored.'' His grip tightened a little as he added, ''I'm not trying to weaken you, Libby. I'm trying to do what's right.''

Her fingers clung to his. ''You'll interfere—''

''I swear I won't. How could I when I have to go back to work soon?''

The remark sent a wave of desolation through her— and the feeling frightened her. She pulled her hand away from his grasp. She didn't want to miss him when he was gone.

He frowned. ''What's the problem? I don't understand.''

Of course he didn't understand. He hadn't built foolish dreams around one night. He hadn't spent days—all right, weeks!—waiting for the phone to ring.

She glanced at him. He'd leaned back in a corner of the booth, resting one arm on the table and the other along the seat. His tanned face wore a concerned look and the deep blue Oregon sky framed in the window behind him was no more intense than his azure eyes.

She stared down at the napkin pieces, and then pushed them aside, scattering the pile she had made. She wanted him gone. She wanted to regain some of the serenity she'd worked so hard to find the last time after he left. She wanted to feel in control of her life again.

So maybe she should quit arguing. Del wasn't like her mother, who used money to tie people to her. For Del, the opposite was true. The sooner she agreed, the sooner he'd leave. She'd simply make sure she accepted his help on her terms. "You'll let me pay you back as soon as I can?" she asked.

He bit back an explitive. "Fine."

"And I still don't want anyone else to know you're the father."

She saw a muscle tense in his cheek, but he didn't argue.

Libby clasped her hands tightly in her lap and drew a deep breath. "Okay, then, I'll quit work. For the next few months *only*, I'll accept your financial help."

7

He'd won, Del realized, meeting her brown eyes. Not only had he gotten her to agree to tell the doctor he was the father, but now she'd also agreed to accept his financial help. "Good," he said shortly. "Let's head back."

It wasn't until they were on the road and halfway home that Del admitted to himself that he still felt oddly discontented. He frowned, thinking deeply while Libby gazed out the window by his side. He felt as if he should do something more. Maybe buy her something before he left. Like a crate of diapers...or formula. He suddenly remembered the article he'd read.

"Are you going to breast feed?" he asked abruptly.

She whirled around, her eyes wide and startled. "Whether I breast feed or not is none of your business."

"I didn't say it was. It's just that breast milk—"

"I know all about breast milk, Del, and you have to stop this before you drive me crazy," she said firmly. "I've agreed to let you help me financially— and we've told the doctor you're the father—but that's where it ends. You promised me you wouldn't interfere."

She was right, of course. He had promised. "Sorry," he said, a bit tersely. "I'm just worried about you—and the baby." The memory of that small, rapid heartbeat echoed in his mind.

She touched his arm lightly—the first time she'd touched him of her own accord since he'd gotten back, he realized. He glanced at her, meeting her softened brown gaze as she said, "You can stop worrying. I have everything under control. Well...except for childbirth classes."

His interest sharpened. Ken and Barbie had mentioned childbirth classes. "Haven't you signed up for them?"

Libby nodded, leaning her head back against the seat. "I did, but now it looks like I'll have to cancel. Christine was going to be my coach..."

Del frowned. Christine, coach? She'd never been on a team in her life.

"...but she's leaving on another buying trip next week."

Del's frown deepened. Which meant Libby would be alone in that big, old house. He'd have to do something about that. He tucked the thought away for future deliberation and returned to the problem at hand. "Isn't there anyone else who could coach you?"

She drew off the ribbon that had loosened from her braid and idly wrapped it around on her finger. "There's someone I thought of asking. I haven't known him very long, but we hit it off immediately..."

She paused, glancing at him fleetingly, and inexplicably Del's heartbeat quickened. Could she be talking about *me?* he wondered.

"The only thing is, he's so busy."

Damn, she *was*. But he needed to get back to Seoul.

"He's really nice—I'm just not sure whether it would be fair to even ask him. I don't want to put him on the spot..." Her voice trailed off.

He'd have to let her down easy, Del decided. He said huskily, "He'd probably appreciate being asked, Libby. Even if he has to say no."

Her troubled frown lightened, and she straightened in her seat. "You're right. Next time I see Dr. Dan, I'll—"

"Dr. Dan!" Del's hands tightened on wheel, and Libby gave a startled squeak as the truck swerved. Swearing under his breath, Del pulled over onto the shoulder of the road and braked to a halt. Clicking off the engine, he turned to face her. "Are you talking about that doctor who tried to pick you up? Why on earth would you ask him?"

"He wasn't trying to pick me up—he was merely being nice, which is the reason I thought I'd ask him. He is a doctor, after all—births aren't anything new to him. He told me once when I ran into him in town that he doesn't have much to do on his evenings off. Since he's a bachelor he'd probably enjoy going to classes with me."

Del's hands tightened on the wheel. Nice? Couldn't she see the guy was on the make? He demanded, "Isn't he on call a lot?"

"I suppose he is—part of the time. But he can't be on call every minute. And since he's new to Lone Oak, too, we probably have a lot in common. We both need to meet more people."

"You don't need to meet more people. You already

know *lots* of people like…like Brooke. Or Susan. Why don't you ask one of them to stand in for Christine?''

''Brooke and Susan have enough to worry about. Brooke is working two jobs to help support her elderly aunt, and Susan is busy with her kids. I'm not going to impose on either of them.''

''Okay, then, what about Mrs. Peyton. She has time on her hands.''

''Mrs. Peyton!'' Libby stared at him in amazement. ''She's very kind, of course, but…''

''But what?''

''She'd drive me crazy,'' Libby blurted out. ''Anyone would be better than her.''

''Fine,'' Del said promptly. ''Then I'll do it.''

If Libby had looked amazed before, now she appeared positively dumbstruck. ''You? But you're leaving.''

Del scowled, even more surprised than she was by his offer. Was he insane? She was right. He had to get back to work.

Libby must have deduced from his silence that he agreed. She sighed in relief. ''Don't worry about it. I honestly don't think Dan would mind—''

Del clenched his teeth. Dan! Why was she so hung up on that damn doctor!

''Don't bother him,'' Del said abruptly. ''I'll take a couple more weeks off and stand in for Christine.''

''But—''

''You're not the only one who can make sacrifices, you know. I'm willing to do my part.'' His eyes roamed over her surprised brown eyes, soft mouth, and down to her rounded breasts and belly. Turning away, he started up the engine. "Simply for the baby's sake, of course."

"I need a couple of weeks. Yeah, John, I know the situation in Seoul is deteriorating—I've been tracking it on the computer. But I have a...situation on my hands here that I have to take care of," Del said into the phone two hours later.

While his boss droned in his ear, Del stealthily opened the kitchen door to the parlor, making sure that Libby or Christine hadn't come back downstairs unexpectedly. After the battle he'd had getting Libby to agree to let him coach her, he definitely didn't want her to hear him arguing on the phone. She'd use it as the perfect excuse to back out of the deal.

No one was around. Del eased the door closed again and turned back into the kitchen. John paused to take a breath, and Del grabbed the opportunity, saying, "You know I've got the time coming. More, in fact."

John yammered on again, mentioning Steve Douglas. Del winced. Douglas, a family man and less willing to travel, was the guy he'd managed to beat out for his last promotion. John was obviously making it clear he was having second thoughts. "Two weeks is all I need," Del repeated. "As soon as I settle things here, I'll be on the first plane out. Count on it."

He hung up the phone.

"Gotcha!" someone said from behind him.

Del stiffened, then turned around. His sister was leaning against the kitchen door, her arms folded over her chest, her jeaned legs crossed jauntily at the ankles. A distinctly smug look adorned her pixie face.

He scowled.

She smirked.

"What are you doing, sneaking around like that?" Del growled.

Her smile widened. "I wasn't sneaking. Libby couldn't find the bear Dorrie Jean gave her so I offered to check to see if it had been left down here. You were just too busy arguing with your boss to hear me come in." She lifted a slim brow. "So what was that all about?"

"Nothing." He glanced around. Spying the bear lying facedown on the kitchen table he picked it up and offered it to his sister.

She ignored it. "Don't give me that. I know what's going on—Libby told me all about it."

His fingers dug into the bear's fur. "She did?"

Christine nodded. She rescued the bear from his stranglehold and put on a solemn look. "I have to say I'm shocked..."

So was Del. He'd thought Libby was going to keep his identity as the baby's father a secret. He opened his mouth to explain.

"It's not like you to volunteer for something as personal as being a childbirth coach—even asking for time off from your 'top secret' job to do it," Christine continued.

Del's mouth snapped shut. He shrugged. "I'm just going to fill in until you get back from your buying trip."

"So Libby told me." Christine combed the bear's fur with her red-painted nails, then paused to admire the effect, adding, "I've realized why you're so willing to help her, you know."

His gaze narrowed on her face. "You have?"

"Of course I have—I'm not a dummy. It certainly wasn't hard to figure out…"

He opened his mouth again.

"It's obvious that the reason you're doing all this is because you're interested in Libby."

His mouth snapped shut. He felt like the dummy—a ventriloquist's dummy, with Christine pulling the strings. He slanted his sister a warning glare. "Stay out of this, Chris."

She looked shocked. "I wouldn't *dream* of interfering. Even though I know that Libby…" Her voice trailed off in a tantalizing fashion. She became immersed in combing the bear's fur again.

Del clenched his jaw to resist the bait. He failed. "Libby *what?*" he asked through gritted teeth.

"You're not interested.…"

He'd strangle her; that's what he'd do. His hands lifted. "Damn it, I'm going to—"

She danced out of reach. "Okay, okay, since you insist." She glanced around the kitchen as if someone might have entered unnoticed, then lowered her voice to a confiding whisper, "I think your chances with her are very, very good."

His anger melted away. Libby must have confided her feelings—her *real* feelings—for him to Christine. "Oh, yeah?" he said, trying to act casual. "Why's that?"

"Because she told me yesterday that she's completely over the baby's father. She must have realized what a jerk he was to leave her in the lurch." Christine beamed. "So don't you see? Compared to him, you'll look good."

His eyes widened—then his mouth thinned. "Thanks a lot."

She smiled sweetly. "No problem. Hey, why don't you take the bear to her? It'll give you a chance to make some points." She handed it over, and with a final pat on the bear's head, she left the room.

Del stared broodingly at the door swinging gently shut behind her. So Libby was completely over him, was she? His jaw hardened. No surprise there.

His scowling gaze fell on the stuffed bear in his hand. He carefully brushed off a bread crumb clinging to the furry little face. The synthetic fur felt soft beneath his fingertips—as soft as Libby's hair. "Quit touching me," she'd said, and the memory sent a small shaft of pain through him. Unlike his sister, he wasn't normally a "touchy" kind of person, but it was so hard to keep his hands off Libby. Stroking her silky hair and satiny skin, holding her in his arms, felt as natural as breathing. Feeling her slim fingers clinging to his...

His eyes narrowed on the bear's blank gaze. That's right. In the restaurant—before she'd drawn away— her fingers *had* clung to his. Would a woman who was no longer attracted to a man do that?

He absently rubbed the bear's furry belly with his knuckles while he considered the question. Maybe it had been unintentional. Or maybe she was just too proud to let him know she still wanted a physical relationship.

Well, one thing was for sure—he had the perfect opportunity to find out.

He tapped Teddy gently on his black button nose. "You know, I'm really looking forward to those classes."

8

Libby wasn't looking forward to the classes at all.

"Seems like a nice place," Del commented as they pulled up before a small brick building next door to the hospital.

She didn't answer.

"Quite a few cars parked out in front," he continued determinedly. "At least we're not the first ones here."

Libby remained stubbornly silent.

Del sighed in exasperation. "Are you going to sulk all night?"

"I'm not sulking," she replied. And she wasn't. She was merely exhibiting her displeasure at his involvement by maintaining a tactful silence.

A wasted effort since Del obviously didn't comprehend the fine shades of meaning exhibited by her behavior. "Sure seems like sulking to me," he said as he climbed out of the truck.

He came around and opened the door for her, collecting the throw pillow she'd grabbed up at the last minute from the couch. "You should have brought the pillow from your bed."

Libby glanced up, her gaze meeting his. Instant heat

flooded her. Intimate memories were in his eyes, and she averted her gaze, placing a hand on her stomach to ease the swooping sensation there. "What's wrong?" he'd asked that long-ago night as she lay naked next to him in the darkness. Brushing back her hair from her damp forehead, he'd gathered her closer to his hard warmth.

"My pillow," she murmured, lethargic from their lovemaking. "I have a hard time getting to sleep without it."

He'd gotten up and found her poor, worn-out feather pillow, and she had thanked him with a kiss that had led to another session of lovemaking.

Her lips tightened. She resented him knowing such personal things about her. She took her sweet time gathering up her purse. She knew her slowness was aggravating him; she knew such behavior verged on the childish. She didn't care.

This was all a big mistake. He might not realize it, but she certainly did. She didn't want him coaching her—not even for a couple of weeks. She didn't want to be in any situation where she was forced into close proximity with Del, remembering things best left forgotten, having him next to her, touching her—like the way he was doing now with his hand planted firmly on the small of her back as he guided her up the walkway.

She deliberately moved away from that unconsciously possessive touch. He cast her an unreadable glance, then immediately looked up as a tall young woman opened the door.

That she was the teacher was apparent as much by the determinedly cheerful smile she welcomed them with as by the impressively large badge proclaiming Amelia Berry, Instructor pinned to her impressively large bosom.

"We're just waiting for a few more couples to arrive," Amelia said, shepherding them into a large carpeted room, bare except for a few straight-backed metal chairs pushed against a far wall along with a large projector. Five other couples were seated in a semicircle on the beige carpet. "I find it creates a more relaxed atmosphere for everyone to sit on the floor," the instructor declared.

Relaxing for whom? Libby wondered as she struggled to lower herself down. Del offered her a helping hand. She sent him a baleful look but accepted it— anything to avoid tumbling over like an unbalanced bowling pin.

Leaving Del to chat with the teacher, Libby smiled at the couples nearby as she tried to get comfortable. Several of the women were sitting cross-legged, a position Libby had abandoned months ago. When the instructor hurried off to greet more arrivals, Del dropped down next to Libby. He must have noticed her shifting and fidgeting movements because he raised his brows. "Why don't you lean against me?"

"No, thank you," she replied primly. "I'm perfectly comfortable." She wasn't, of course, but she finally found a halfway bearable position by tucking her legs to one side.

She tried to relax. All the other women looked so serene and well-dressed. Libby tugged on the hem of her shirt. She hadn't been in the mood to shop for anything new. Maybe she should have worn her denim jumper, but she was so tired of the outfit, especially since a faint pink stain remained on the breast where she'd dropped the icing during her shower. Appreciating her dilemma, Christine had produced the blue pin-striped men's shirt Libby now wore, declaring that it would do perfectly well as a maternity shirt when teamed with navy blue pants.

Libby hoped her friend was right. At least the shirt more than amply covered her. It hung well past her hips and she'd cuffed the sleeves neatly to her elbows. The only place the shirt was a little tight was across her breasts.

She nervously fingered the button there to make sure it hadn't come undone and Del leaned closer, his warm breath brushing along her neck as he drawled, "That's my shirt, you know."

"No!" Taken by surprise, Libby's eyes widened. "Christine said she found it at a thrift shop."

"That's her euphemism for my closet," he said dryly. "She constantly pilfers my clothes and then conveniently forgets where she found them."

"I'm sorry. I'll return it as soon as we get home," Libby said stiffly.

"Don't bother." Reaching up, he smoothed down her collar. She could feel the warmth of his hand as his knuckles brushed her cheek. "You look pretty in blue," he said quietly.

Although she frowned and moved away from his hand, something inside her seemed to glow at the comment. Disturbed by the realization, she welcomed the distraction as Amelia entered the room again, followed by the couple from the doctor's office. "Everyone's here now, we're ready to get started," the instructor said, clapping her hands lightly to draw everyone's attention while Ken and Barbie found a spot across the room to sit down.

"Why don't we all take turns and introduce ourselves?" Amelia suggested, smiling brightly. "Include your due date and whether you're expecting a boy or a girl."

Libby's heart sank. She hated doing this sort of thing. She concentrated on the other couples, trying to decide how much she'd say when her turn came. The women did most of the talking with an occasional comment from the men. Libby mentally categorized the couples as she listened.

The "Been-there-done-that" Benedicts, were having their fifth child and wore almost identical expressions of bored exhaustion. Next in line were Howard and Linda McLean, who resembled nothing so much as a husband and wife cheerleading team. After each of Linda's breathless chants of information, Howard would chime in with a brisk, "That's right!" pumping a muscular arm for emphasis. The next two couples looked alarmingly young, but both were married, Libby noted, her anxiety increasing as her turn approached.

When the woman next to her shyly finished speaking, Libby drew a deep breath. Before she could begin, however, Del spoke up. "I'm Del and this is Libby," he said abruptly. "Our little girl is due in October."

"Our *boy*," Libby blurted without thinking. She bit her lip as his eyes gleamed with satisfaction, while across the way Ken and Barbie exchanged a knowing glance.

"Oh, are you expecting twins?" asked the female cheerleader.

"No!" said Libby horrified. Goodness, she wasn't *that* big, was she?

Amelia must have noticed her dismay because she said soothingly, "Libby is one of the farthest along. She and Del are taking the class a little later than most." The instructor smiled at the Pattersons. "Your due date is the next closest on our list."

Barbie smiled complacently, placing a hand on her stomach, while Ken introduced himself and his wife. "I'm a dentist and my wife is a child psychologist," he added, passing out their business cards. "It's a good idea to have your baby psychologically assessed as soon as possible. The birth process can be traumatic. And, of course, you should have their teeth checked as soon as they come in. We now have special braces that—"

"Thank you, but we'd better get started," Amelia said, interrupting his sales spiel. She then launched into one of her own, explaining the class would be covering "self-awareness, self-control through programmed exercises, and reduction of pain through education and knowledge of the labor and delivery process."

She started with a lecture on the baby's developmental stages inside the womb. Libby listened intently for a while, but soon found her attention wandering. She'd already read extensively on this topic—nothing new here. She glanced at Del. He was leaning forward, his gaze fixed intently on the teacher. Good Lord, he was even taking notes! He'd pulled a crumpled envelope from his pocket and was scribbling as fast as he could on the back.

Libby swallowed her rising misgivings. He was really getting into this stuff. When Amelia mentioned the benefits of breast over bottle feeding, he even gave Libby a nudge and an "I told you so" glance. You'd think he'd personally invented the process, she thought indignantly.

She brooded over his interest awhile, but soon more pressing matters occupied her mind. She needed to go to the bathroom. Was the woman ever going to stop talking? she wondered in growing alarm. To make matters worse, the baby woke up and began kicking her swollen bladder with disturbing frequency.

Finally, Amelia paused reluctantly for a break. Libby levered herself up and raced for the bathroom, managing to beat the other women to the single stall.

Emerging triumphantly a few minutes later, she returned to the classroom and headed immediately for the chairs. Even the cold, hard metal felt good after sitting on the floor for an hour, an opinion apparently shared by most of the other women who soon joined her. Only the cheerleader and Barbie disdained the relative comfort, returning to sit stiffly upright on the floor. All the men remained standing, clustered in small groups, but Libby noticed Del had cornered the teacher and appeared to be grilling her on some point.

Del didn't have time to get all his questions answered, but by the time the break ended, he was definitely a proponent of breast feeding. When the instructor clapped her hands to herd her flock back to their pillows, he glanced around for Libby and spied her sitting on a chair, gripping the bottom on either side as if she thought someone might take it away. Striding across the room to her, he put out his hand

and hauled her to her feet. "Come on. They're ready to start again."

She dragged her feet following him and, glancing back, Del suppressed a smile at the sight of her forlorn face. She wasn't enjoying this, he knew. During the lecture she'd shifted around repeatedly, trying to get comfortable. But he was thankful that they'd come. "Our" baby, she'd said—before the entire class. Satisfaction filled him and he tightened his grip slightly on her slim hand. For the first time, Libby had admitted in public that the baby belonged to him, too.

"You'll like this next part," he promised, helping her sit down again. "Amy said—"

"Amy?"

"The teacher," he explained in response to her questioning tone. "She told me to call her Amy. Anyway, she said that for the rest of the evening we'll be practicing relaxation techniques."

Libby didn't look reassured. If anything, her expression changed to one of trepidation. He led her to a fairly secluded corner of the room when Amelia directed in crisp tones, "Spread out, everybody. Now the first thing I want you to do is learn to relax at your coach's touch."

Libby acquiesced in the first exercise with fairly good grace, flexing and relaxing the muscles in her arm at his command. But the second exercise didn't go well at all.

"Ouch!" he said, jerking away from her fingers on his arm. "You pinched me!"

"You pinched me first."

"I was *supposed* to pinch you—Amelia said to. To help you learn to relax against the pain. And I certainly didn't do it as hard as you did to me," he added, rubbing his sore skin.

"I don't care. I don't want to be pinched at all—and certainly not in preparation for more pain. What kind of perverted reasoning is that?"

He tried to explain it to her, but finally abandoned the attempt as Amelia clapped her hands again. "Attention, everybody. Our time this evening is almost up and I like to end the classes with a relaxation meditation and massage you can practice at home along with your breathing techniques. Mommies, lie on the floor—on your right sides, please!—and, coaches, sit next to them and follow my instructions."

Libby didn't want to lie down. Del could tell by the way her slim brows lowered over her eyes and her mouth turned pouty. But she finally did so with a sigh, turning on her side with her back toward him.

Miss Berry dimmed the lights and switched on a cassette. A familiar sound in Oregon—the rain trickling through the trees—filled the room. "Now, coaches, let's begin with a simple massage of the shoulders. Gently work the tension from your partner..."

Partner. Del liked the sound of that. Whether she liked it our not, for the next couple of weeks, he was Libby's partner in this baby business. Placing his hands lightly on her shoulders, he gently kneaded her rigid muscles.

Feeling her stiffen, Del's satisfaction faded. So she didn't like his touch. Setting aside the hurt frustration her action caused, he patiently persisted in the massage. Gradually she relaxed beneath his fingertips, and soon she looked almost asleep. Her thick lashes drooped heavily over her eyes, her hair tumbled lazily across her pinkened cheek. Even pregnant, her waist dipped inward when she was lying down, and his gaze slowly roamed the feminine curves of her breasts and hips revealed in the shadowy room as he worked.

"Move to the arms," Amelia chanted softly, her voice almost blending with the background serenade of raindrops. "Gently massage down to the fingers."

Libby had slim arms and delicate wrists. Faint blue veins pulsed beneath her skin there and he had the urge to kiss the sensitive spot.

"Don't neglect the fingers..."

He didn't neglect the fingers. He massaged the pad of her thumb and the hollow of her soft palm. He rubbed her small fingers, bending them gently.

"Let's do the calf muscles. Pregnancy often causes sudden cramping in this area."

He loved her legs. Long, slim, with nicely defined calves; ankles so small he could easily encircle them with his finger and thumb.

"Now the lower back," Amelia instructed. "This is where most pregnant women feel the greatest strain from the weight of the baby."

Del obediently moved his palm down to Libby's hips and lower back, pressing carefully with the heel of his hand. She sighed a little, her eyes fluttering shut, and something inside him eased on a wave of tenderness. Wanting to comfort her, Del kept up the soothing motion. The span of his hand easily encompassed the width of her back, and he could feel the delicate ridges of her spine through the thin cotton of her—*his* shirt.

He smiled faintly. He liked it when she wore his clothes. She'd been wearing one of his shirts the first night he'd met her, when he'd inadvertently startled her in the hall as she came out, damp and fresh from her bath.

She hadn't known *that* shirt was his, either. She'd clutched the neck in an instinctive gesture of feminine alarm. The material had pressed across her breasts, revealing the circular shadows of small dark nipples.

Had her nipples changed? he wondered now. Were they darker, bigger, *sweeter,* than they'd been before? The position in which she lay had caused the top couple buttons of her shirt to come undone, while a third strained across her plump bosom. His brooding gaze lingered there, craving a glimpse of the soft skin he'd kissed and caressed.

"Okay, Mommies, roll to the other side."

Libby turned over, her movements slow and lethargic with the heaviness of relaxation. She looked tousled and sexy, her eyes drowsy, her lips red and full.

As she lay down again, the button across her breasts gave up the battle. Her shirt gaped open. Involuntarily, Del's hungry gaze fastened on the plump curve of her breast. A nipple pressed against the thin lace of her bra in a rigid peak. Surprised at the small sign of arousal, his glance shot to her face.

For a brief moment, her unguarded gaze met his. Her eyes were slumberous, filled with remembered passion. Then she flushed, and her lashes fell, shielding her gaze as she reached up to clutch the front of her shirt closed.

Del's body hardened and his gaze narrowed on her averted face. Had he imagined the desire he'd seen there?

He put his hand on her ankle. She flinched, then

froze, like a little rabbit caught in a trap. Beneath the
fan of hair on her cheek, her color deepened, and her
breath emerged between parted lips in short pants.

His own breathing quickened in response. So she
felt it, too—this desire that sparked between them.

Suddenly, the lights went on. Libby pulled free of
his grasp and sat up. "That's it. We're done now."
She rose to her feet. Del did too, reaching out a hand
to help steady her, but she avoided his grasp and hurried toward the door, holding her pillow in front of
her like a shield.

Del remained where he was, watching her, a small
smile curving his lips. *No, we're not done yet, Libby,*
he promised silently. *We're not done at all.*

9

Was Del pursuing her?

The question flashed through Libby's mind with increasing frequency and alarm during the rest of the week.

Most of the time she was able to scoff at the notion. Why would he be? He'd accepted the situation between them. He was satisfied with the financial agreement they'd reached, and was allaying his conscience further by taking her to the childbirth classes.

At the thought of the classes, her nipples tightened. She couldn't help remembering how good his hands felt stroking her skin. It has been so long since she'd been touched...which was probably the reason she was overreacting. It wasn't as if she were any kind of femme fatale, after all—especially almost eight months' pregnant. She had three outfits to her name, her skin was blotchy and her breasts and belly were huge. Hardly any man's idea of a dream lover.

No, she was imagining his interest, she'd tell herself. But then she'd look up suddenly from frowning over her knitting, or gazing out the window at the falling leaves, and she'd find his eyes fixed on her with the same hungry, sexual intent that she'd seen at that class—and so long ago during that storm.

Sitting on Christine's bed, watching her friend pack for her flight that afternoon, Libby said, "I wish you didn't have to go," and then bit her lip. She hadn't intended to voice the thought. The words had slipped out unintentionally.

Christine looked up in faint surprise. "I'm sorry, too, Libby, but you don't have to worry. I know you'll be safe with Del here."

As safe as a mouse in the care of a hungry cat, Libby thought ruefully. She glanced down at her stomach. A fat, clumsy mouse at that.

Christine added, "I hope he doesn't get called back unexpectedly. His beeper's gone off a couple of times, and it seems to me he's been getting a lot of calls the past few days."

Libby had noticed that, too. She'd answer the phone and a clipped, hard masculine voice would demand, "Mr. Delaney, please." Del took the calls in the study, and every time he came out, Libby waited for him to say, "I need to get back right away. Something's come up," the way he'd done the morning after they'd made love.

"Where is he now? Working on his computer?" she asked. All the time he'd been gone, the computer had sat lifeless in a corner of the study. Now, however, Del had booted the system up, spending hours working in front of the blue-lit screen.

Busy pawing through a pile of hosiery to find the unruined pairs, Chris answered absently, "He went out to the hardware store to get a new faucet for the leaky one in the kitchen and was waylaid by Susan, who persuaded him to come over and take a look at her new Jacuzzi.'' Glancing over at Libby, Christine wrinkled her nose with a wry grin. "She made it sound as if it were broken, but that's just an excuse to get Del alone. Ever since her divorce, she's been chasing him almost as avidly—but a lot more subtly—then Mrs. P. does for Dorrie Jean."

Which put her own worries in perspective, Libby thought. Feeling a sudden need to be busy, she refolded Christine's favorite blue dress. Christine declared the thin blue sheath was uncrushable, but Libby couldn't believe the fine, silky material would benefit by being wadded into a corner of the suitcase the way Christine had done. She laid the now neatly folded dress in the case. Why would he still be interested in her when Susan—with her slim, blond good looks— was available? He'd accepted that Libby wanted a husband who was around all the time; she'd accepted that he wasn't going to give up his job. No, like he'd said. He was simply staying for a little while for the baby's sake.

She maintained that belief on Monday, since nothing changed much with Christine gone other than Del's sudden interest in her eating habits. He arrived to oversee her consumption of "the proper nutrients" at breakfast, lunch and dinner, but otherwise left her pretty much alone while he fixed various things around the house. In the evening, when she sat down with her knitting before the television in the parlor, he disappeared into the study, saying he had reading to catch up on.

On Tuesday, he caught her standing on a chair, while she searched for a mixing bowl in a high kitchen cupboard. He lifted her down and handed her the bowl along with a few choice remarks. She'd simmered with anger the rest of the day, but arrived at the conclusion that no man who claimed a woman was a "little idiot" could possibly be interested in her.

On Wednesday, the firmness of her conviction wavered a bit when he unexpectedly brought her roses—huge, beautiful pink blooms. "The color matches your cheeks," he said, thrusting the fragrant mass into her arms. Her suspicions rising, she might have accused him of flirting with her if he hadn't added, "I always pick a bunch up for Christine when I'm in town. She gets a kick out of them."

Okay, so he equated her with his sister. That thought reassured her through Thursday—until their childbirth class that evening. Libby sat through a video of an actual birth in growing alarm. Thank goodness Del wouldn't be around long enough to really go through the process with her. She'd *never* let him see her looking sweaty and desperate like the woman on the screen. Why, Libby wondered, had she never noticed before how *big* babies' heads were?

She expected Del to be disgusted by the film; instead, he was fascinated. The cheerleading couple, who'd originally answered all the teacher's questions, could barely get a word in edgewise between Del's quick replies. Did he spend *all* his time reading pregnancy books?

Later, as they went through Amelia's "relaxation massage," she glanced covertly around. None of the other coaches' touches seemed to affect the women the way Del's affected her. Under his hands her skin flushed and tingled, her nipples hardened with excitement. Was it her imagination, or did his fingers linger as they stroked her legs, climbing toward her hips and buttocks? When he massaged her arms, she glanced sharply at his face. Had she imagined the brush of his thumb against her breast? The innocence in his expression *seemed* genuine....

And she believed *that* up until Friday night, when she returned from a long evening walk and an unexpected run-in with Mrs. Peyton. By the time Mrs. P. had grilled her on her weight gain, eating habits and even more personal topics, Libby had been more than thankful to escape into the house.

Unsuspectingly, she walked through the kitchen and pushed open the dining room door. She froze, looking into the shadowy room.

There were candles on the supper table.

Flames danced atop the slender white tapers, casting a flickering golden glow over the table set for two. No light shone from the electric chandelier. Only candlelight glinted off the silverware and the creamy white china. A single yellow daisy nodded lazily in a glass of water.

Libby tried to swallow. Her mouth felt dry. She'd seen this scene before. Her mouth felt dry and her palms grew damp. Even the delicious smell of roasted chicken was familiar. Her heart began thumping in slow, painful beats. This was the exact same scene she'd created the night she'd decided to make love with Del.

"Hello," he said behind her.

She whirled around. He was standing close—too close.

"Oh! Hello. I didn't see you there," she stammered, taking a nervous step away. "Let me get the lights."

She lunged for the switch on the wall.

Click. Click—click. Nothing happened.

She stared at the switch. "It seems to be out," she said, her voice hollow.

"So it does. Good thing I got out the candles," Del said cheerfully. "Come on and sit down, while I bring in the food. I have everything ready."

He did. Roasted chicken and mashed potatoes. Sweet green peas and baby carrots. Even a luscious double-chocolate cake for dessert.

"More chicken?" he asked, politely proffering the platter.

"No, thank you." She could barely finish the piece she had. He'd cooked the bird perfectly, roasting it to a smooth golden brown. Much better than the slightly burned one she'd made for dinner months ago that they'd laughingly demolished with their fingers.

"How 'bout carrots?"

"Love them," she said brightly. They hadn't had carrots at the *other* dinner—the only vegetables she'd been able to find in the pantry were canned green beans. Del loved green beans; she hated them. But she'd eaten one off his fork when he'd coaxed her to and been rewarded with a slow, lazy smile that had made her breath catch.

"Mashed potatoes?"

"Umm, thanks." She pushed them around, sculpting a small mountain on her plate. Not one lump! He'd claimed her lumpy potatoes were full of "substance."

She refused the cake, ignoring his lifted eyebrows. He knew she loved chocolate. She'd insisted on making "s'mores"—the one talent she'd emerged with after a two-year stint in the Girl Scouts—and had piled the chocolate bars high between oozing melted marshmallows they'd toasted in the fireplace. The marshmallows had dripped on to her fingers. Del had sucked the stickiness off each one.

"Are you sure you won't try a piece?" he asked. He forked up some cake, gooey with icing, and held it temptingly close to her lips.

"Well…" She hesitated. It did look good. The thick icing swirled around the top of the rich, moist bite of forbidden pleasure.

Her lips parted.

"It's delicious," he murmured. "Susan brought it over."

Libby's head jerked back. The fork wobbled. Icing plopped down on her breast. "Oh, no!" Libby said, staring down at the glob.

Quickly, Del reached over. Scooping the icing up, he popped it in her mouth with his finger. Her lips closed automatically over the tip. His skin felt excitingly rough against her tongue. Her nipples puckered.

His eyes, staring into hers, dilated.

Pushing his hand away, Libby jumped up, scrubbing furiously at the spot with her napkin. "I told you I'm not hungry!"

"At least not for food," Del murmured. His eyes were half-shut, filled with a slumberous satisfaction as he leaned back in his chair.

Libby threw down her napkin and fled to the parlor. Night had fallen in earnest now, and only a few small candles glowed in the darkened room. She considered snatching one up and going upstairs, but reluctantly

abandoned the idea. It would look too much like flee-
ing. She didn't want Del to know how his presence
alarmed and—oh, all right!—excited her, too.

She hurriedly reached into the sewing basket by the
chair, arming herself with her knitting. She'd keep the
conversation impersonal—no more suggestive com-
ments.

Del strolled casually into the room. Barely sparing
her a glance, he went over to the fireplace, crouching
down to light the logs piled on the hearth. The tangy-
sweet scent of pine filled the room.

"The days are getting chilly again," he said.

"I know. I've started putting extra blankets on the
bed." She bit her tongue. Why did she have to mention *bed*, when that was the last subject she wanted
brought up?

Sure enough, he turned her way. Worse yet, he rose.
Libby's pulse quickened as he slowly walked toward
her. He looked big and broad—and dangerously sexy
outlined by the growing glow from the fireplace behind him.

He leaned over her. Funny how in the darkened
room her other senses felt heightened. She could feel
the warmth of his body, hear the steady hush of his
breathing, smell the enticingly musky scent of his skin.

It had been like this before—during the blackout.
The same, almost painful awareness had shivered
through her body, tightening her nipples, flushing her
skin. She held her breath…then released it with a gasp
as he reached into the basket next to her chair. He
pulled something out and dropped it in her lap.

Libby picked it up. Pink booties. She frowned in

confused surprise. "They're darling. Did Christine make these?"

"I did."

"You!" She stared at him in shock. "I didn't know you could knit."

"There's a lot," he drawled, echoing her words, "that you don't know about me."

Libby studied his handiwork. The rows were neatly even, the corners straight. "How did you learn to knit so well?"

He dropped into the wingback chair next to hers, slinging a long leg over the plump arm. "Mom taught me one winter along with Christine—probably to keep us from tearing around the house so much. She fooled me into thinking we were tying fancy knots. By the time I realized it was 'sissy stuff,' I'd already learned the basics."

"Christine's never mentioned it," she said faintly.

"I swore her to secrecy as a kid—under the direst of penalties." His eyes narrowed. "I guess I'll have to swear you to secrecy now, too," he said softly.

Her fingers clutched the booties. She didn't want to share a secret with him. She didn't want to share *anything* with him.

Her face must have revealed her thoughts, because he leaned closer, his eyes reflecting tiny flames from the fireplace. "Do you swear?" he whispered menacingly. "Or do I have to tickle you into compliance like I did with Chris when she was six?"

"I swear," she promised hurriedly.

He grinned and moved away a little. She lifted her chin, recovering her composure. "Like I said, these are very nice." She added kindly, "Too bad they're pink. I'm having a boy."

"A girl."

"A boy!"

He eyed her thoughtfully, then suddenly reached over and plucked her knitting from her hands.

She gave a startled squeak. "What—"

"I think you need a break," he said, smoothly overriding her protest. Standing up, he grabbed her hands and pulled her to her feet. "Come on, let's practice that relaxation massage Amy taught us."

"No, thank you. I am relaxed," she said through gritted teeth, trying to loosen his grasp.

"This will help you even more," he promised. He pulled her over to the fireplace, grabbing a couple of pillows to put down on the rug. "Sit down—"

"I don't—"

"Sit *down*."

She sat down. "You're so bossy," she said as he hunkered down behind her. He began to work her shoulders. She stiffened at first but soon relaxed a little. He was massaging just the right spot. To hide her pleasure, she added in a grouchy tone, "I *knew* that you would be."

"And you're pretty irritable. You should have eaten more."

She bristled, hunching her shoulders under his hands in annoyance. "I *did* eat. I just haven't been very hungry lately."

He kept rubbing rhythmically until she relaxed again, her tension easing. "I know you haven't been hungry," he said. "Which is why you might consider taking two prenatal vitamins—like the doctor suggested—instead of only one.''

Libby glowered at the fire. She hated those horse pills. They made her gag, they were so big. She opened her mouth to tell him so and he added, ''For the baby's sake.''

She subsided. ''Okay,'' she said grudgingly. He knew that she'd do anything for the baby.

Silence fell between them, broken only by the crackling of the burning pine logs. Del continued the massage. As his warm hands stroked her skin, drugging relaxation seeped through Libby. Her insides felt as if they were melting, but her nipples tightened into aching peaks. She stared into the fire, her eyes drooping half-shut.

He gave her a little push, silently urging her to lie down. Libby obliged, curling on her side with an arm beneath the pillow under her head. He shifted position, lifting her foot into his lap. His thumbs firmly stroked the pad of her foot through her sock. Warmth from the touch of his hands on her sole seemed to travel up to her thighs. When had he taken off her shoe? she wondered.

She shifted, planning to ask him, when a yawn caught her by surprise. She patted her mouth, saying, ''Oh, pardon me.''

''I noticed you've been pretty tired lately,'' he commented. ''Maybe you should consider taking a nap in the afternoons.''

Libby frowned. She didn't like to sleep in the daytime; she never had. She started to tell him so, when he added, ''For the baby's sake.''

His thumb stroking the arch of her foot felt so good.

Libby decided not to argue. "Okay," she mumbled, "for the baby's sake."

The fire glowed warmly on her face and stomach. Del's strong, warm fingers dug into her calves, chasing away the tightness there. She blinked lazily at the fire. It was getting harder and harder to keep her eyes open.

"Libby…"

"Hmm?"

"I've noticed you've been tense lately. I can hear you pacing at all hours."

His thumbs softly rubbed the sensitive skin behind her knees, and Libby stirred, his touch causing a corresponding tingling achiness between her legs. He started on the back of her thighs, pushing aside the hem of her jumper to stroke her bare skin. Libby sighed. She hadn't realized how much she ached there. She didn't want him to stop. The firm circular motion was turning her muscles into mush. His hands moved higher.

He added, "The books I've been reading say a wholesome physical relationship is the best cure for stress."

"Um-hmm…" His hands felt so good on the top of her thighs. She stirred again. Unconsciously parting her legs a little, she shut her eyes, concentrating on the melting sensation his touch invoked.

"So I think we should make love…for the baby's sake." His hands moved higher. He massaged her buttocks.

"Okay." She moaned. "For the—" Her head jerked up. She glanced swiftly around. "*What* did you say?"

10

His hand still rested on her bottom. Suddenly becoming aware of that fact, Libby scooted out of reach, picking up a pillow to hold in front of her.

He watched her calmly. "You heard what I said."

She clutched her pillow tighter. "I don't want to make love."

"Why not?"

"Why not?" She stared at him. "It's obvious why not."

"Not to me, it isn't." Reaching out, he took her hand in his, gently toying with her fingers. "So tell me."

"Because, ah..." The reasons were obvious—so much so that she couldn't remember them for a moment. She was distracted by the feel of his thumb, rubbing her wrist in small delicate circles. Was it the candlelight that softened his expression so? If only he'd stop staring at her with that tender yet intent look in his eyes. "What was the question again?" she asked vaguely.

The tenderness crept into the small smile he gave her. "I asked why you don't want to make love," he repeated patiently.

Libby blinked. "Oh, that's right. Well, because I'm pregnant for one thing."

"So? Pregnant women make love all the time. The doctor even told you it was okay."

"But think about what happened the last time."

His grip on her hand tightened. "I am thinking about it."

The hungry note in his voice caused Libby to think about it, too. Heat burned under her skin from her breasts to her cheeks. "I'm *talking* about the fact that I got pregnant."

"Which is something we certainly don't need to be concerned with *this* time."

She said weakly, "It wouldn't be right..."

"I'd make it right."

The hard certainty in his tone made the muscles in her stomach clench. Her fingers tightened on his. He would make it right—like he'd done the first time when he'd lured, demanded and cajoled her body into responding to his. By the end of their lovemaking, she'd been limp with satisfied exhaustion.

A woman couldn't ask for a more caring and experienced lover—during the limited time he'd be around.

"No," she choked out and yanked her hand out of his.

She headed almost blindly toward the door, only to be brought up short by his firm, "Wait!"

She hesitated instinctively at the command in his voice, then watched him uncertainly as he strode over to the light switch on the wall. He flicked it up and the lights in the hall and parlor blazed on.

Libby's eyes widened. "I thought we had another power outage!"

"Nope, just a loose bulb in the chandelier."

Her hands fisted at her sides. "You tricked me!"

He shook his head. "I never said the power was out. You just assumed it."

"Neglecting to say something can be as big a lie as telling an untruth."

He lifted an eyebrow. "I agree...especially in view of what you haven't said."

She didn't want to ask the question—something in his expression told Libby she'd regret it—but she couldn't stop herself. "What do you mean?" she demanded.

His eyes held hers. "I mean in your entire list of reasons why we shouldn't make love, never once did you say that you didn't want me."

Libby fled up the stairs.

Three hours later, lying alone in the darkness, Libby finally admitted the truth: Del was right. She wanted him.

A light rain pattered outside. She turned over, trying to find a comfortable position in the big bed. Her sheets felt hot and wrinkled, the covers too heavy. Her skin felt sensitized and she rubbed her wrist, as if the feel of Del's callused fingertips lingered there.

It didn't make sense to be so physically attracted to him. Logically, she knew he wasn't the safe, steady man she should want. But her body didn't seem to be reacting to logic, but rather to the memory of how it had felt to make love with him the last time, to have his hands and lips moving gently over her, leading her to a soaring ecstasy she'd never known even existed.

She moaned. Rolling onto her side, she yanked her pillow from beneath her head and hugged it to her, trying to relieve the sexual pressure peaking her nipples and causing a melting readiness between her thighs. Darn him for reminding her how it had felt to make love. Darn him for showing her that he remembered, too.

Because now she couldn't forget. She felt restless and tense, filled with the same urgent desire that had driven her into his arms and bed eight months ago.

Sitting up, she gave her pillow a few good whacks, then lay down on it again. He made it sound oh-so-easy. Make love—relieve the itch—and then continue on as if nothing had happened.

She flopped over onto her other side. It just wasn't possible....

Her eyes popped open. She stilled, staring wide-eyed into the darkness. Or was it?

She sat up, absently rubbing the satin edge of the blanket between her finger and thumb as she considered the question. It wasn't as if she was the naive little fool she'd been before, after all. She knew his job came first with him; she knew that wouldn't change. But so what? She had plans of her own about the kind of man she wanted and needed for the long-term. She couldn't get hurt this time because emotionally she was completely over him. All she needed was to overcome this physical craving, too.

She frowned. But maybe she'd been going about this thing all wrong. Instead of keeping him at a distance, maybe what she needed was a good dose of Del.

Maybe she should take him—just once more—as kind of a lovemaking inoculation shot. Not enough to make her lovesick again, just enough to make her immune.

As he'd pointed out, she was already pregnant—that wouldn't change. The doctor had said sexual relations were okay; the pregnancy books even encouraged intimacy, saying it was a good method of alleviating stress—and heaven knew, she felt stressed.

So what was stopping her?

She shoved her blanket aside. She'd do it. She'd make love with Del, yet maintain complete control, curing her desire for him once and for all. This time she'd simply refuse to let any emotional nonsense confuse her.

Kicking away the rumpled covers, she started to step out of the bed. Her toes had barely brushed the rose-colored rug when she paused, doubts overtaking her again. She placed a hand on the round ball of her belly. Who was she kidding? Did she really think she had the nerve to waddle into Del's room, eight months' pregnant, and ask him to make love with her? Never mind that he seemed to want her, too. He didn't know how much her body had changed under this prim white nightgown.

She sighed. She just couldn't do it. She sat there forlornly, her legs still dangling. Suddenly a small furry body with tiny claws scampered over her foot.

Libby's scream was long, piercing and instinctive. She leapt to the center of the bed. By the time Del pounded his way up the stairs and burst into her room, she was still standing there, clamping her nightgown around her thighs as she alternately covered one bare foot with the other.

"Watch out!" she shrieked, and Del whirled around, muscles tensed and fists up in an automatic fighting stance, ready to take on the unseen opponent hiding in the darkened room.

"No—over there!" she called.

He spun again, biting out, "Where? I can't see him."

"I think he ran under the bed."

About to lunge in that direction, Del paused. "*Ran* under the bed? What the hell am I fighting?"

"A mouse."

He stood frozen a moment before the tension eased from his muscles and his fists dropped. He ran a hand through his hair. "Good God, you scared the sh— dickens out of me."

"Well, he scared me," Libby said defensively, still standing with one raised foot tucked behind the other, like a disheveled stork. "I can't sleep in here with him running around."

"So sleep somewhere else."

It sounded reasonable. The only trouble was, Libby had developed a distinct aversion to stepping on the floor. Finally, after several attempts to get her down had resulted in no more than a series of squeaks and continued foot hopping, Del literally took matters into his own hands and bundled her into his arms.

He was wearing only boxers, and the smooth skin of his chest and shoulders felt warm against her. Startled, but too relieved to protest, she threw an arm around his strong neck as they began walking. "Wait!" she cried suddenly when they'd made it half-way to the door. "My pillow. The mouse might try to nest in it or something."

Del obediently turned back to the bed, bending with a slight grunt to enable her to pick up her pillow.

"And the baby's clothes," she remembered when they were on their way again. She lunged forward to try to scoop them off the dresser, causing Del to stagger slightly at the unexpected shift in weight. "And—"

"That's it," he said firmly, heading out the door. "It's a mouse, for God's sake, not a rabid wolverine. It's not going to destroy everything in sight." He managed to hit the hall light switch with his shoulder. Light flooded the hallway and he started down the stairs, maneuvering his bulky burden around the landing corner, swearing when his elbow hit the railing. Libby's death grip tightened around his neck. He choked out, "Can you lower the pillow? I can't see."

"Oh. Sorry." Libby's grip eased and she tried to get down.

But he didn't want to let her go. She was cuddly and warm in his arms, and her sweet-smelling hair brushed his cheek. Del held her tighter and quickened his pace.

Automatically, her arm curved behind his neck again. He strode down the hall, saying to distract her from his destination, "I didn't know you were afraid of mice."

"I didn't, either," she admitted. "But I've never had one run across my foot like that before."

He walked into his bedroom. "I'll trap it tomorrow."

"Oh, don't," she said anxiously, gazing up into his

face. "I don't want you to kill it—just relocate it somewhere."

"Like a government witness, huh?" he said dryly. "Fine. I'll try to catch it and relocate it in the woods. But until then, you'll be safest right here." He lowered her onto his bed. "Under my...protection."

11

Libby lay back against the pillows. The sheets were still warm from his body. Trembling with nervous anticipation she pulled the covers up to her chin. "I don't think we should do this."

Moonlight filtered in through the window, gleaming off Del's smooth muscles as he stripped off his boxers and climbed in beside her. "I definitely think we should."

Libby could see the hungry desire etched on his face as he lay, propped on his elbow, looking down at her. She swallowed nervously and his gaze fastened on her mouth.

He bent, his lips slowly closing over hers as he enveloped her in his warm embrace. Libby's eyes fluttered shut. Del was such a good kisser. He tasted like coffee and mint toothpaste. He kissed her lightly at first, seeming to savor the taste of her, too. Then his tongue engaged hers in a teasing battle that quickly turned serious. He kissed her deeply, demandingly, until nothing existed except his hungry mouth.

Libby felt dizzy with an exhilarating breathlessness. Her muscles tensed in anticipation while her insides seemed to melt into liquid warmth. She wanted this—

she wanted him. But when he reached for the first button on the neckline of her prim nightgown, her hand covered his, stopping him from unfastening it.

His fingers stilled. He lifted his head to study her worried expression in the shadowy darkness. "What is it, Libby," he whispered. "Don't you want me?"

"It isn't that..." How she wished it were that simple.

"What, then?" he coaxed. He pressed a kiss against her temple.

"It's just..." He met her gaze. She couldn't hold his intent stare. Her eyes shied away. "I don't look the same."

He lifted his hand and gently tilted her chin up to meet his gaze once again. He regarded her solemnly. "These big brown eyes look the same," he said softly, dropping a kiss on her fluttering lashes. "And this nose—" another kiss landed there "—is just as cute as ever."

His gaze lingered on her mouth. His voice thickened. "These lips don't taste any different." He pressed several kisses there, until her lips were swollen and moist, her chest rising and falling with her quickened breaths.

Still kissing her, his hand trailed down to her breasts. Barely lifting his mouth from hers, he murmured, "Now *these* feel very different." He carefully cupped a swollen globe, weighing it in his hand. He smiled against her lips. "But it's not a difference any red-blooded American male is likely to complain about."

He palmed her puckered nipple and Libby moaned with almost aching pleasure. He smiled again. "You still like that, do you, sweetheart?'' he murmured. Bending his head, he dropped a kiss on each peak through the thin cotton.

His hand glided lower over her belly, delicately molding the firm roundness. Through the gown, his finger circled her belly button—once an ''innie,'' now an ''outie.'' ''This is different, too—much, much different. But this—'' his hand moved lower, sliding beneath her gown to nestle in the curls between her legs ''—*this* feels very familiar.''

Libby closed her eyes, writhing a little at the restless yearning growing with his teasing touch. This time when he tugged her nightgown slowly upward, she didn't resist, but raised her arms to help him.

He tossed the gown to the floor. She lay there beneath his gaze, achingly aroused, achingly vulnerable. His face tautened. ''Oh, Libby—'' He reached up to cover her breast. ''How beautiful you are.''

She wasn't beautiful, but she felt so under his eyes and hands. He gently kneaded her swollen flesh, brushing his thumb firmly across one taut nipple. She gave a little cry, his touch sending lightning stabs of pleasure along her nerves, increasing the liquid warmth between her thighs. As if he knew, his hand moved there.

Her fingers dug into the hard muscles of his arms to push him away—to draw him closer. She remembered the sharpening need, the rising crest of desire— but had his touch been so tender before? So confidently sure of how to wring the tiny gasps of satisfaction from her lips?

His warm breath flowed across her cheek as he

breathed, "Do you like this, Libby? Am I hurting you at all?"

"No," she moaned, but she *was* hurting because she had to hold back; she couldn't get lost in his arms again. His hand swept along the sensitive curve of her bottom, and she clenched her fingers in the sheets to keep from stroking him, too—to keep from becoming absorbed in the salty taste and musky scent of his skin. She fought to ignore the huskily murmured endearments that he groaned into her neck.

"Oh, sweetie, you feel so good, so soft. So tight."

She moaned again as he explored deeper, her senses spiraling higher and higher. In an urgency of need, she tugged mindlessly at his shoulders, trying to urge him over her, but he rolled onto his back instead, carrying her with him. He gripped her buttocks in his big hands. "Come on top of me, love," he coaxed, "so I don't hurt you."

She did, climbing on him to ride the tightening spiral of desire, his rocking body carrying her upward until the darkness burst behind her eyes in a shower of stars. She cried out. He did, too.

Libby's body felt weightless, floating down from the heights. For just a little while afterward, she savored the feeling as she lay cradled in Del's arms, listening to the beat of his heart beneath her cheek. Then she carefully moved out of his hold to lay down on her side, facing away from him.

He immediately curved his body around hers, pulling her back until her bottom rested against his lap. His hairy, muscular leg bracketed her smooth one. His big hand splayed on her belly. This time Libby waited until his deep even breathing told her he'd fallen asleep, before she eased away from his touch again.

She shivered as she moved to a cool spot on the sheets, resisting the urge to snuggle close to his warmth again. She'd done it, she told herself, ignoring the tears that burned behind her eyes. She hadn't run her fingers through his hair, or traced the contours of his strong back or muscular buttocks. If a tiny part of her had wanted to cling a bit tighter, soar just a little higher, she'd managed to prevent it, to stay in control.

There would be no repercussions this time. No way that she'd get caught.

12

↤←

Libby felt hopeful the next day, in control of things again. Her confidence was strong enough that when Del went out to rake the fallen leaves, she did something she'd been delaying for the past seven months.

She went into the silent study. In the corner, Del's computer hummed quietly. Turning her back on the faceless machine, she picked up the phone and dialed the 213 area code and Liz's unlisted number.

Nervously twisting the cord around her finger, she waited the prerequisite fifteen minutes from the time the housekeeper answered until Liz came on the line. Liz never came to the phone right away. Ever conscious of her image, she wanted to make sure the caller was aware that she was a very important, very busy woman.

"Oh, hello, Elizabeth," she drawled in response to Libby's greetings, a faint hint of disappointment in her voice. The media calls Liz had once been bombarded with were coming fewer and farther between. "I didn't realize it was you. How are you surviving in the wilds of Oregon?" In Liz's opinion the only states worth bothering about were the ones with film studios.

"I'm fine, Liz. In fact..." Libby took a deep breath. "I'm pregnant."

There was silence on the line. Libby's stomach knotted and she twisted the cord tighter around her finger as she waited in nervous uncertainty for her mother's reaction. When Liz laughed, the famous, husky laugh so familiar to her fans, Libby's throat tightened in disappointment.

"Now that's something I didn't expect," Liz drawled. "If you were sixteen, yes, but twenty-something? I can see our little talk about the facts of life is long overdue." She paused. "Are you going to...take care of it?"

"If you mean am I planning on an abortion, the answer is no," Libby said bluntly. She rested a comforting hand on her belly. "But I am planning on taking care of my child myself."

"How admirable of you, darling. But all alone? Where's the dear daddy?"

"He's around. But we're not involved." Libby pushed the picture of exactly how involved they'd been last night from her mind.

"Isn't that just like a man—you can never depend on them. What's that old saying? Why buy the milk when you can get the cow for free?" Liz chuckled.

Libby discovered she'd wrapped the cord so tightly that her finger was turning white. She loosened the coils, adding, "Yes, well...I just wanted to let you know you're going to be a grandmother."

"Oh, my God!" For just a second, Liz's voice turned shrill with honest horror. "I can't be a grandmother. I'm only..."

"Forty-nine."

"Forty-one," Liz snapped. "Do you think that producer would have called me for the part of a young mother if I'd been that old?"

Libby didn't bother to argue. Nothing would ever make Liz admit to her real age—or the fact that producers no longer cast her in such a role. She'd convince herself that one had, and then manufacture some "crisis" to excuse herself from taking the mythical part. How complicated it was living in the fantasy world her mother constantly created.

Libby listened to her mother's monologue about the new film without comment, however, until Liz concluded, "So, you'd better come home."

"No," Libby said. "I'm staying here."

"Darling, be reasonable. I need you." Liz's voice altered again, assuming the exasperated yet loving tones of a good parent. She was very convincing in the role, Libby thought idly. After all, she'd been perfecting it before the media for years. "Besides, how are you ever going to be able to take care of an infant on your own?"

Libby refused to let doubt weaken her. "I'm not coming back, Mother," she repeated.

Liz sighed. "Then my best advice is to make him marry you, darling. You have the perfect weapon—guilt. Believe me it can work like a charm. And even if the marriage doesn't last, at least you'll seem a little smarter—and you'll get some alimony."

"I don't want a temporary marriage. I want the real thing."

"It's a little late for that. If he'd wanted to marry you, he would have asked you before you got pregnant, don't you think?"

Yes, I do, Libby thought, ending the conversation and hanging up the phone. She stared at the screen saver on Del's computer—colorful little stars exploding on a dark background—while she thought about what Liz had implied. Guilt had made Del offer to marry her; guilt was keeping him in Lone Oak. Before Liz's reminder, she'd almost been in danger of forgetting that—especially in his arms.

Maybe it wasn't a good idea to have a physical relationship with him...and yet, could she resist? She sighed. She hadn't managed to so far. She'd simply have to keep reminding herself that this was a purely physical affair.

No love allowed.

Libby was eluding him.

The suspicion crossed Del's mind with increasing frequency during the next few days.

At first he scoffed at the notion. How could she be? They'd finally made love again—and he planned to continue doing so every chance he could. She slept with him every night. How could she be withdrawing from him, when in bed he held her as close to his heart as any two people could be?

No, he had to be imagining her aloofness.

He maintained the belief without effort on Monday. He felt so content; he didn't want to let Libby out of his sight. They spent the misty day puttering around the house, going out in the afternoon to the nearby woods to free the little mouse he'd managed to capture.

In the evening he talked her into going out for dinner. They'd driven all the way into Grant's Pass for a cozy meal at the Yankee Pot Roast. He thought she would enjoy the quaint brick restaurant, created from a Victorian house—and she had. Afterward, she refused to let him buy her flowers at a nearby florist, but when they got home, he managed to coax her into bed for some "extra rest." They didn't come out of his room until late the next morning.

Tuesday afternoon he was full of energy; Libby seemed the tiniest bit irritable. Despite his orders not to bother, she insisted on straightening the house. When she came into his room, he caught her up in his arms and laid her down on the bed. She immediately tried to rise again, and he gently shoved her back down. He sat beside her, capturing both her hands in his to keep her in place.

She narrowed her eyes at him. "Let me up, you...you...big oaf."

He lifted his brows in pretended astonishment. "Is that the best you can do? Good Lord, not only are you cranky, you also have a limited vocabulary."

"I am *not* cranky!"

He shook his head sadly, trying not to laugh at her outraged expression. "Yes, I'm afraid you are. I hope our daughter isn't listening. Let's find out." Releasing her hands, he gently laid his ear against her stomach. "Support Crew to Mission Control. Can you hear me in there?"

"For goodness' sake..." Libby gave his shoulder a halfhearted shove.

He ignored her, saying, "Wait! I've gotten through. I think she wants to tell us something."

"*He*—I mean, oh, get away from me."

Del lifted his head and regarded her sternly. "Stay

still. All this wriggling around is causing static." He put his head against her again, apparently listening. "What? What's that you say? Mom's grumpy because she hasn't had sex in twelve hours? Tsk, tsk."

This time Libby pushed him so hard he slipped off the bed. "Sexual deprivation is *not* my problem," she said, her lips primly pursed.

He climbed lithely to his feet. "Nor mine, either—after last night. No, I think *your* problem is you need a nap. Why don't you take one while I start dinner?"

"I'm not even tired," Libby said, with just the hint of whine in her voice. She must have heard it, too, because she winced and conceded, "Okay, I'll lie here for a few minutes."

When he checked on her two hours later, she was still sound asleep, her hand tucked under her cheek. He covered her up—intending to leave her alone the rest of the night. But when he started to straighten, she'd reached up, tentatively touching his bare shoulder, and he laid down beside her, forgetting his good intentions.

On Wednesday Susan called to ask him to fix her malfunctioning garage door opener. He hadn't wanted to go, but finally agreed when Libby kept urging him to. Faintly piqued at her lack of jealousy, he'd spent an hour on the ten-minute job, hoping she would miss him—then spent two hours pacing the house when he got home, until she returned from a walk to the library. She seemed surprised at his concern, and politely declined his suggestion to let him know where she'd be the next time she went out. His annoyance with her lasted until evening. He finally forgave her when it was time to go to bed.

On Thursday morning they had decided to go shopping when the phone rang. Libby didn't complain when he disappeared into the study to handle the call from his supervisor, and ended up working on the computer for a solid three hours. Afterward, though, she seemed a little quiet as they scoured the stores to find what she called "exactly the right color for the bassinet cover." After waiting twenty minutes while she vacillated between yellow and green, Del pressed her to make a choice.

To his shock, she suddenly burst into tears. He took her into his arms. She was trembling a little, and he pressed his lips against her forehead, trying to comfort her. She sighed and rested against him a moment, before pushing gently away to stand on her own two feet. Despite her protests, he bought her both covers and rushed her home and back to bed. For once he didn't join her. Instead, he brought up her favorite peanut butter and banana sandwiches on a tray, heroically refraining from grimacing while she ate the loathsome combination.

Later that evening, she insisted on going to their childbirth class. During the break, the women headed for the chairs, even Barbie no longer disdaining the relative comfort. Soon everyone was discussing baby names. The Benedicts admitted they were open to suggestions. Linda and Howard had narrowed their list down to Troy, Bubba or Dion.

Barbie ran a complacent hand down her beige silk maternity smock. "*Our* precious darling will be Kenneth Iven Patterson, Jr.—after his father," she announced. "Kenneth means 'handsome one' and Iven means 'little yew-bow.'"

The group made suitably admiring noises except for Del. "Kip," he said, standing next to Libby's chair.

Barbie glanced in his direction, her smile fading. "I beg your pardon?"

"The other kids will probably call him Kip—because of his initials," Del elaborated. "Or maybe Junior or Butch."

Barbie's expression said clearly "over-my-dead-body" before she smiled sweetly. "That's an interesting thought. So, what are you planning on naming your little boy—girl?"

Del glanced at Libby. She hesitated. "I was thinking of Nicholas—after my father."

Barbie clasped her hands together. "How...cute. Although he might get called St. Nick. Are you sure you don't want to call him—what is it?—Delbert? After his father?"

Libby merely shook her head.

Del drawled, "My name isn't Delbert."

Libby didn't say much after that, nor mention the conversation on the way home, but later, as they lay in bed together, she brought up the subject. The covers were tucked up to cover her bare breasts, her hair fanned out over her pillow. Hazy moonlight filtered in through the open curtain, faintly illuminating her solemn expression as she asked, "You're a junior, too, aren't you, Del? I think Christine mentioned once that you're named after your dad."

Del was lying on his side facing her, propped on his elbow as he lazily sifted her hair though his fingers. At her question, he let his fingers drift down along the smooth warmth of her cheek to her mouth. Idly tracing the plump curve of her lower lip, he admitted, "Actually I'm the fifth Delaney to be saddled with the family name. My great-great-grandfather started the tradition of sticking the firstborn son with a tag that the kid spends the rest of his life either trying to hide or fighting over."

She smiled faintly and ran a finger along the bump on his nose. "Christine says that's how you broke your nose—fighting with a kid who teased you over your name. She says since then she hasn't dared tell anyone else what your real name is."

He tapped her nose back in teasing warning. "Because she knows she'll be in big trouble if she does." His thumb gently brushed Libby's lower lip, back and forth, before his hand slid lower to tilt up her chin.

His gaze met hers. He murmured, "Only the people who really love me are allowed to know my real name."

Libby stared silently up at him, her big eyes searching his in the semidarkness. Del waited, his muscles tensing in hope and anticipation. *Ask me,* he urged her silently. *Come on, Libby. Ask me my real name.*

She didn't speak. Anticipation ebbed away and an ache grew in his chest. When she started to move away from his touch, his grip tightened and his mouth closed fiercely over hers.

He kissed her without stopping, exploring the soft skin of her cheek, the sharp edge of her teeth, the exciting, faint roughness of her shy tongue. He kissed her until her breath came in short pants and her arms curled tightly around his neck.

Moving lower, his lips roamed the sensitive column of her neck, the hollows in her shoulders. He delicately tasted her so-sensitive nipples and the ripe curve of her stomach. Down, down he moved, gently nipping her thighs until she shivered with excitement, then he kissed his way to the curls at the apex of her thighs, ignoring her dwindling protests and concentrating instead on the feel of her hands in his hair, clutching him to her—the sound of her satisfied moans as she climaxed.

Overwhelmed by a sudden fierce need to be inside her, he moved back up and behind her, pulling her into his arms. He entered her carefully, tenderly, moving slowly until the tension built and her muscles tightened, until she writhed and moaned in his arms. He couldn't get close enough, couldn't hold her tight enough to him as they moved together in an ever-increasing rhythm. His muscles clenched, sweat built on his body. It felt too good. He fought to hold back the feeling bursting within him, and finally her muscles squeezed him in tiny spasms.

His groans of completion mingled with her soft cries. Spooned together, his body still curved around hers, they lay together as their breathing slowed.

When he held her in his arms, whenever they made love, everything felt right with the world. Full of contentment, Del had almost drifted off to sleep when he felt Libby ease out of his hold. An odd emptiness growing inside him, he watched from beneath lowered lashes as she moved to the far side of the bed and turned away with a sigh.

She'd been turning away a lot of times lately, he realized suddenly. In bed and out.

Long after she'd fallen asleep, Del lay with his hands linked behind his head, staring up at the dark ceiling. He couldn't kid himself any longer; things still weren't right between them.

He'd thought if he could get her to come to him, their problems would be resolved. He'd thought if he could get her back into his bed, everything would be like it had been before—the first time they'd made love.

But it wasn't. Libby was friendly enough, but there were no more of those deep, soul-satisfying conversations like they'd had those few far-off days when they'd first met—when they'd been completely honest with each other, revealing things they never had before. Oh, she talked—she especially talked about the baby. Her future plans for him, how she'd take care of him. But she wasn't asking for Del's advice or including him in those plans. She'd be able to share the same things with a chance stranger she'd met on the streets—like that damn doctor, he thought with a sour taste in his mouth.

Del suspected she no longer wanted to share anything intimate with him at all. Even during lovemaking, he was always aware that she was holding something back, keeping a part of herself aloof. It baffled and enraged him. But what really hurt was the way she'd move away afterward, placing a careful distance between them in the bed. It was as if that foot or so of empty white sheet negated what they'd just shared.

His jaw clenched and he sat up. Well, it wouldn't work—not anymore. He reached over and carefully drew Libby's limp, sleeping form into his arms. She snuggled her head on his shoulder and draped a leg and arm across him. He dropped a kiss on her soft hair.

Holding her close, he tried desperately to think of a way to get her to abandon this game she was playing. They weren't strangers; they were lovers. She belonged to him.

The firm curve of her stomach pressed against his hip. The baby kicked faintly and Del placed his hand against the tiny movement. The baby belonged to him, too.

His eyes narrowed. Maybe that was the problem. As long as she refused to admit the baby was his, Libby was able to pretend that they weren't as involved as they were. Once she admitted to everyone the baby was his, would she still feel such a need for distance? Probably not. But could she be persuaded to admit to everyone that he was the father? He doubted it.

So maybe she'd have to be trapped into the admission.

A small smile played at the corners of his mouth. He hugged her a little closer. This time he'd make certain Libby was well and truly caught.

They were caught late the next morning lying in bed as Christine and Dorrie Jean walked past the open bedroom door.

Del watched from beneath half-closed lids, his arm draped around Libby, as the two women paused in the hallway, identical expressions of shock on both faces.

He had heard them coming. Christine's chatter, as she unlocked the door downstairs a few minutes earlier, would have been hard to miss. When he heard them climbing the stairs, Chris complaining all the way to Dorrie Jean about the weight of her suitcases, he'd started to wake Libby—only to think better of the idea. This might be the opportunity he'd been hoping for. If his sister and Dorrie saw them in bed, Libby couldn't deny her involvement with him any longer....

At that moment, Libby turned and cuddled closer, sealing her fate. Del decided to wait just a few minutes more.

His sister blurted out, "Omigosh!" before Dorrie managed to yank her out of sight. That ought to do it, he thought. Now to wake up Libby.

"Sweetheart..." he crooned softly in her ear.

She scrunched up her face in annoyance and burrowed farther into her pillow.

He waited a few seconds and tried again. "Libby..." The pink lobe of her ear was too tempting. He nibbled on it gently.

This time she responded. She gave a husky chuckle, while at the same time snuggling her bottom more firmly against him.

Gallantly, Del resisted her unspoken invitation. "Libby," he murmured a little louder, "Christine is home."

"That's nice." Libby sighed, pillowing her cheek on her hand. "Tell her—" She jerked upright. *"What did you say?"*

He met her gaze calmly. "I said Christine is back from her trip a day early."

"Oh, no," she moaned. Pushing her hair out of her face, she searched frantically through the rumpled bedclothes. "Oh, no," she said again and began tunneling her way beneath the covers to the foot of the bed.

Del regarded the wiggling lump of her bottom with interest. "What're you doing? Trying to hide?"

"Don't be silly! I'm trying to find my nightgown. I need to get out of here before Christine sees me."

"She's already seen you." He added on an afterthought. "Dorrie Jean, too."

The lump under the bedclothes froze, then moaned again. "Oh, no!"

"Yep." Del stretched luxuriously, yawning hugely. Scratching his chest, he glanced around and caught sight of Libby's nightgown on the floor next to the bed. Stealthily, he snaked his leg out from beneath the covers into the cold morning air and hooked the gown on his toe. Hauling it up, he hastily stuffed it under his pillow. He leaned back, linking his hands behind his head just as she popped up from beneath the covers again.

"Where could it be?" she wailed, holding the blankets to her chin.

He shrugged.

"There it is!" She pounced on a bit of lace poking out from beneath his pillow and pulled the gown out. Del sighed regretfully, hastily assuming a surprised expression when she glanced his way. "How on earth did it get there?" she asked suspiciously.

He innocently spread his hands, palms up. "I have no idea."

Still holding the bedclothes up over her breasts, Libby struggled into her nightie. "You think they saw us?"

"Yeah."

Her anxious face pushed through the neck opening. "You're *sure?*"

He pictured Christine's astounded expression. "Very."

"Well, what are we going to do?"

"What can we do but go down and say hello? We can't stay up here all day." He swung his legs out of the bed, standing up for another stretch.

Libby quickly averted her eyes from his nude form—then snuck a quick peek. Although she'd tried to hide it, she never could resist looking at him.

Catching her studying him, his gaze heated. "Unless you *want* to stay up here…"

Her fists clenched as she looked pointedly away. "How can you joke?"

"It's not the end of the world, Lib." He pulled on his jeans, buttoning them as he turned to face her. "Get dressed and we'll go down and face them together."

"No. Not now. Not together." She envisioned Christine's shock, her own humiliation.

His brows drew together and he placed his hands on his hips. "Are you ashamed of being seen with me?"

"Yes." His scowl deepened and she added hastily, "Oh, not with you per se, but what are they going to think? Here I am—pregnant—and already in bed with who they believe is another man."

"So we'll tell them the truth—that you've only ever slept with me and that's my kid you're carrying."

"I can't do that—I don't want to do that. What would everyone say?"

Del shook his head in exasperation. "Who cares?"

Libby gazed at him, her eyes stricken. "I do."

Softening a bit at the distressed look on her face, Del added, "Don't worry about it. Run along and get dressed. I'll go down and explain.'' He headed to the door.

"No! Maybe I can convince them not to tell anyone.''

He paused. "Dorrie Jean won't tell anyone.''

Libby looked up hopefully. "She won't?''

"Nope.''

His tone was so definite Libby relaxed a little—only to tense again as he added, "Christine will, though.''

She shoved at the covers. "I have to stop her. Don't say anything until I get there.''

"Libby…'' He gave her a reproachful look. "Don't you trust me?''

Before she could answer, he strode out the door.

Libby hurried to stop him, but by the time she made it into the hall, he'd already disappeared down the stairs. She raced up to her bedroom, threw on some clothes and dashed down again, entering the kitchen in a breathless rush.

Christine and Dorrie Jean both glanced up at her arrival. Chris was sitting with both elbows leaning on the table, while Dorrie Jean appeared to be edging toward the door.

Dorrie Jean put her hand on the knob. "Hello, Libby. Sorry to have, uh, woken you up.'' Her face flamed with embarrassment. "I'd better get home now. Mother is waiting for me to drive her to her pedicure.''

"Let me walk you out, Dorrie,'' Libby said, ignoring Del's bland look and Chris's surreptitious wink. "I want to talk to you a minute.''

They both stepped outside on the sunny back porch, and Libby closed the door firmly behind them. She was considering how to phrase what she wanted to say when Dorrie Jean said shyly, "I'm so happy for you, Libby."

"You are?" Libby bit her lip. "Uh, what exactly did Del tell you?"

"Just that he's asked you to marry him and that you're still trying to make up your mind. I think you should say yes."

"Oh, Dorrie…" Libby said helplessly. "You must think I'm terrible."

"Of course I don't." Dorrie picked up a burgundy maple leaf that had fallen onto the wide porch railing. She twirled it between her fingers, sending Libby a fleeting glance. "I—I'm glad that you and Del have gotten together," she said haltingly. "He's a nice guy. He never made fun of me, like some of the other guys did in school. Once, he even took me to a prom. Mother asked him to ask me, I know, but Del never let on. He pretended it was all his own idea."

Dorrie met Libby's gaze, a rare smile lighting up her solemn gray eyes. "Everyone was always doing that to Del—his mom, Christine, even the other women in the town. They all take advantage of his niceness, his sense of responsibility. I've often wondered if maybe that wasn't part of the reason he stays away so much from Lone Oak."

She shyly touched Libby's arm. "He must really care for you, Libby, if he's willing to take on the responsibility of another man's child."

An unexpected lump clogged Libby's throat. *He doesn't care for me,* she wanted to respond. *I'm just a responsibility, too.* Instead, she swallowed, saying softly, "It's a bit more complicated than that. I really would appreciate it if you wouldn't tell anybody what you saw.''

"Of course I won't.''

"Thanks, Dorrie.''

Libby watched Dorrie Jean leave through the picket gate, then walked back into the kitchen with a sigh. Christine was no longer there. Del, busy cracking eggs in a big yellow bowl, glanced up to ask cheerfully, "One egg or two? I'd better make it two," he decided before she could speak. "You didn't eat much last night.''

"I'm not really hungry," Libby said, but knew it would make no difference. He'd make the eggs, anyway. "Where's Chris?''

"Probably on the phone, spreading the good news.''

"Oh, my God—" Libby started to rush out of the room.

He caught her arm lightly to stop her. "Whoa, slow down there. I was just kidding." Although he was smiling slightly, his eyes held an intent look as he added, "Besides, would it be so horrible if I wasn't?''

"Yes," Libby said unequivocally. "You don't want to be tied down—not really." As he opened his mouth to interrupt, she added, "And I want something more in a relationship than good sex.''

His eyes narrowed, his mouth flattening into a thin line. "At least you acknowledge we have that much," he drawled. "Don't be so quick to knock good sex.''

"I'm not," she answered just as lightly. "But I'm not going to base a major life decision on it, either.''

She strolled out of the room, hiding the sudden shakiness she felt inside. She found Christine upstairs unpacking her suitcases.

Christine pounced as soon as Libby entered the room. "Great!" she said, her eyes lighting up. "I was hoping you'd come up so we can talk. I don't have much time—I'm flying out tomorrow morning."

Always on the go. Just like her brother, Libby thought with faint weariness. Why couldn't these Delaneys stay in one place?

"Libby…" Christine touched her gently on the shoulder. "Are you all right? You look a little pale."

"I'm just tired," she said automatically.

She immediately wished she could call the words back. Chris's blue eyes gleamed. "I can understand why after seeing you and my brother in bed together."

Libby's face flushed. "Which is exactly what I came up here to talk to you about—"

"Go ahead! I can't wait to hear the details," Chris said, throwing several blouses from the case onto the floor. She picked one back up, clipping it on a metal hanger. "I had no idea you and my brother had gotten together."

"We haven't." Libby sat down at Chris's dressing table. Pushing aside the plethora of makeup littering the surface, she propped her elbows on the table to rub her temples.

Christine shot her a disbelieving look. "Oh, c'mon. I'm sorry Dorrie Jean and I embarrassed you, but you were in bed together."

"That was just one of those spur-of-the-moment things."

Christine's brows drew together over her eyes in a way that was disconcertingly like her brother's. "I don't believe it," she said bluntly. "I know my brother is no saint, but he would never take advantage of you simply for a sexual relationship.''

''He didn't. If anything, I took advantage of him—oh, please, Chris, do you mind if we don't discuss this anymore? All I want is your promise you won't tell anyone what you saw.''

Christine's eyes widened in hurt surprise. ''Why of course I wouldn't tell anyone—not on purpose, anyway,'' she added conscientiously. ''I promise I'll try extra hard not to let anything slip.''

But if Libby thought that would end the matter, she was very much mistaken. Until she left the next morning, Chris continued to badger her about Del every chance she had.

''He cares about you, Libby,'' she claimed as they did dishes that night. ''I'm sure of it. He worries about you all the time.''

''He bosses me around all the time,'' Libby corrected, wiping a plate delicately detailed with soft pink roses. ''Your brother is a take-charge kind of guy. It's second nature for him to tell people what to do.''

Chris plopped more dishes into the soapy water. The old-fashioned sink was a deep one and water sloshed up past her elbows as she groped around the bottom. ''We need a dishwasher,'' Chris grumbled as she did every time she washed. She returned to the subject at hand. ''It's more than him just being bossy,'' she insisted stubbornly. ''He told me he wants to marry you—''

''Chris! I don't think you should discuss this with him.''

''I didn't discuss it with him,'' Chris declared, washing a handful of silverware. ''I just told him what

I thought—and not in as much detail as I wanted to since he was busy on the phone again..."

He's always on the phone, Libby thought. He'd have to be leaving soon.

"...but he said *you're* the only one against marriage..."

The traitor! Libby fumed.

"And if that's because you think he doesn't love you, Libby, you have to be wrong. He must love you if he's willing to take on another man's baby," Chris added, unconsciously echoing Dorrie Jean.

A band of pain seemed to squeeze Libby's heart. "He doesn't love me." She wiped a plate, put it down and picked up another. "He's never said he loves me. *And,*" she added a little louder as Christine tried to interrupt, "even if he did, I still wouldn't marry him. I want a real father for my baby—one who's there for him all the time. I know from personal experience how hard it is to only see your dad once or twice a year."

Chris hadn't said any more, but Libby knew she wasn't happy with the situation. Until she left for her plane, Chris kept sending her reproachful looks. Despite their bickering and teasing the Delaneys were close. Christine obviously couldn't understand why anyone would pass up her brother.

It should have been easier when Christine left again. It wasn't. Libby thought at first he might try to renew their sexual relationship. She wouldn't let him, she decided. But when an entire week passed and he made no effort to do so, she felt oddly upset.

Brushing her teeth early one morning, she considered possible reasons for his change in attitude. Maybe he'd had second thoughts about their liaison since

Christine and Dorrie Jean had caught them. Maybe he was simply sexually sated; he didn't need her anymore. She paused in her vigorous brushing. Or maybe he was turned off by her altered appearance.

Mouth full of foam, she studied her reflection. Like the rest of her, her face had grown rounder. For a while—before Del's return—her cheeks had seemed to sink in a bit, giving her rather an interesting look. Now, with all the rest she'd been getting and Del's constant monitoring of her diet, her cheeks had plumped out. Like a chipmunk, she thought. She puffed them out to heighten the effect. Yes, definitely chipmunk material.

She spit and rinsed, and studied herself again. Her hair had changed, too; it seemed much limper than before. Maybe it would look better if she put it up. That might make her cheeks look less round. She lifted her hands, gathering her hair on top of her head—and immediately dropped her arms again. The pose had accentuated her breasts and belly to an alarming degree. Slowly, she turned to the side to study her silhouette. No getting around it; she was huge. Behemoth. Ready to join the circus as a walking bowling ball. It was a miracle her legs could even support her. Her figure had to be the reason Del had lost interest.

She plucked at her jumper in dissatisfaction. These maternity clothes didn't help, either. She was heartily sick of wearing a tent every day, but she could no longer tolerate even stretch pants. The elastic chafed her stomach. She'd tried pushing the band beneath her stomach, but then had to worry about them sliding off completely. Maybe Del, accustomed to his style-conscious sister, was simply tired of looking at such a fashion failure like herself.

She went down the stairs, unconsciously looking for him, only to discover he was holed up in the library again. She frowned. Maybe the problem was simply he was too busy, too anxious to get back to his work, to think about her. She pressed her ear against the paneled door. *Solar listening post, communication upload burst, infrared tracking* and other technical phrases filtered through the wood. Libby hurried away into the den, feeling absurdly guilty. It wasn't as if she were a spy or anything, but how would she explain her actions if he suddenly came out?

Was he ever coming out?

She sat down in her favorite wingback chair with a sigh. It wasn't as if she missed him or anything; she had plenty to do. After all, the baby would be arriving in less than a month now. Desultorily, she picked up her knitting from the basket. She'd simply gotten used to spending a lot of time with him. Knit, purl. Not only that, but he *had* promised to help her get that bassinet down from the loft in the garage. Knit, purl. Knit, purl. No doubt he'd forgotten. *He* had more important things to worry about.

She sniffed. Not like *her*. Knit, purl, sniff. All *she* was good for was having babies and knitting booties— and she wasn't very expert at either of those things. Her ankles were swollen; she couldn't get comfortable. Her back had been killing her since late last night. But did he care? Oh, no. Knit, knit, sniff, sniff. You'd think the least he could do would be to get off the phone. Would it kill him to pay her a little attention? He'd certainly been eager enough to when she'd first met him, when he'd wanted sex. Now that she'd grown swollen and ugly, he couldn't be bothered. The yarn blurred. A wave of self-pity caused tears to burn in her eyes. She wallowed in the emotion, knitting blindly along until the bootie was a hopeless tangle of knots. That made her cry even harder.

By the time Del found her half an hour later, she was sitting in her chair, her eyes and nose red from crying over the mess of yarn in her lap.

He paused in the doorway a moment, silently assessing the situation. He'd noticed over the past week that her moods were becoming increasingly erratic— just like the pregnancy books had warned. He would have to proceed cautiously. "Is something wrong, Libby? Commercials getting to you again?" He cast a knowledgeable glance at the television. "Nope, TV's off. Which means you must have forgotten to eat breakfast. You know that always makes you irritable."

Libby stiffened in righteous indignation at the callous remark. Okay, maybe she had cried over a commercial once or twice—the one with puppies was a real tearjerker—and no, she hadn't eaten. But how dare he accuse her of being irritable when she'd sat here with almost saintly patience, waiting for him to get down that bassinet?

She told him all this in no uncertain terms as he pulled her to the kitchen.

"I know, you're right—I have the sensitivity of a rock," he agreed absently, peering into the refrigerator. "We'll get the bassinet after you eat something… Ah, ha! Here's the milk."

"I don't want any," she declared, turning up her nose.

"Have some while I make your sandwich," Del ordered.

He waited a moment to see if she wanted to argue further, but she must have recognized he meant business. She followed him to the table, watching with a disgruntled look while he poured a tall, cold glass.

He put it into her hand. She took a sip, then another, pausing to give him a speculative look. "All of it," he said firmly.

She wrinkled her nose and tilted the glass, downing the rest in three long gulps. Gasping slightly, she slammed the glass down and glowered at him. "Are you satisfied now?"

Del met her angry gaze. She had a faint milk mustache above her pink lips and her brown eyes were snapping. No, he wasn't satisfied. He hadn't been completely satisfied since that night eight months ago.

He'd been disappointed by her refusal to admit the truth to Christine and Dorrie Jean, but her stubbornness only made him more determined than ever. He'd left her alone this past week, hoping that she would miss him, would give some sign that she needed him, too. But every day she seemed to be drifting farther away. He was tired of waiting…and he was running out of time. In three short days he was due back in Seoul.

He caught her in his arms. Her brown eyes widened. She opened her mouth to protest, but his lips covered hers, stifling the sound in her throat. She tasted sweet—like milk and Libby. His tongue explored her mouth with thorough domination.

Then he let her go.

Swaying a little, she blinked dazedly up at him, her

lips still moistly parted, her hands still clinging to his shoulders. Del glared down at her. Did she think she could find this with anyone else? Did she think that he would let her?

He pulled her close again, murmuring in her ear, "Let's go to bed, Libby. You need a nap."

It was exactly what Libby had needed to hear—an hour ago. Now the words filled her with rage. Did he think he could ignore her for a week and then just sweep her off to bed? She pushed away from him. "A nap, huh? Give me a break. Is that all I am? A convenience for you?"

Del's anger, tightly controlled for the past week, suddenly surged to meet hers. "If you think there's anything convenient about this arrangement, then think again. I'm staying here to help you out, and all you can do is snap at me."

Libby wanted to cry—but darned if she'd give him the satisfaction. "Nobody asked you to stay. In fact, why don't you just go right now."

"Maybe I will."

"Fine."

"Fine!" He stalked back into the den.

Head held high, Libby marched out the back door. The arrogant swine! Acting as if she was the one who'd asked him to stay, when really it had been all his idea.

She didn't need him. She didn't need any man. Not for anything. She jerked on her padded coat and headed to the garage, her fists clenched at her sides. If that was his attitude, she'd darn well get that bassinet down by herself.

The wooden garage door was old and heavy. Libby

heaved it up with one mighty tug. The ache in her back lanced around to her side but she ignored the pain, scanning the neatly arranged garage.

There it was. She could just see the bassinet up in the loft, resting under a stack of boxes. The loft itself wasn't too high. Only about three feet higher than the hood of the truck parked neatly beneath it.

She couldn't find a ladder, but she refused to give up. She should be able to get up there no problem at all, she decided. She'd simply climb on the truck hood, get the bassinet and climb back down again. Nothing to it.

She put her foot up on the front fender. It was hard—much harder than she'd expected—to hoist herself up. She bounced up and down, trying to get some leverage, with no results.

She frowned. Maybe she should try tackling the problem from another direction. She turned around and backed toward the vehicle. After just three tries, she ended up sitting triumphantly on the hood.

Now to stand. She tried—and slipped. She fell back, her coat padding her fall. More surprised than hurt, Libby lay there a moment, her legs dangling over the front fender. It wasn't until she tried to sit up again that she discovered the full extent of her problem. She couldn't get up. Like a turtle flipped on its shell, the weight of her belly and the padded coat kept her pinned in place. She tried rolling to one side, then the other. She tried sliding forward. Finally, she resorted to wiggling and flapping, trying to inch her way down.

She was still flapping when Del found her. "Libby! Oh, my God, are you hurt?"

Embarrassment, not pain, kept her from answering

for a moment. She took a deep breath. "No," she admitted gruffly. "I'm stuck."

"You're lucky you didn't break your neck. You *knew* I'd get that down for you." His tone was harsh, but the arms scooping her up were gentle. He lifted her against his chest and Libby's arm automatically encircled his strong neck. She peeked at his face and much of her embarrassment faded. He sounded angry, but his expression was positively stricken. White lines edged his mouth and his eyes were dark with worry.

He must care a little bit, Libby thought. All at once, the thought of him leaving, of not being there for the birth of the baby, seemed too much to bear.

Her arm tightened, and he stared intently down into her face. "You're so pale. Are you sure you're not hurt? I think you should go to the doctor's."

"Of course I don't need to see a doctor," Libby said, slightly mollified by his concern. "I just slid down—I didn't fall. I'm perfectly—uh-oh!" Her eyes widened.

"What is it? What's wrong?" Del demanded.

But by then he knew.

"My water broke," Libby said in a small voice.

13

 ◄—

"I hate you!"

"I know."

"I really, *really* hate you!"

Del's mouth quirked wryly. "Right now I'm not liking myself too much, either."

Libby probably would have responded, but the pain that held her in its grasp peaked at that moment. Her face contorted in agony. The fetal monitor strapped around her belly uttered encouraging quick beeps that finally slowed to a steady hiccup as the cramping gradually subsided again, and the once fairly rational woman Del had brought into the hospital reverted to the virago she'd become after eighteen hours of labor.

"I don't like anything about you. Your shoulders are too broad, you're too tall—and your hair. I hate the way it always falls right into place. It's so…thick," she said in a disgusted voice.

Del ran his hand through his offending hair. "Sorry about that."

Blocked on that point, Libby glared at him fumingly. The pain was coming again. She could feel it gathering low in her belly. "I don't like your nose, either," she panted. "It's not straight."

"It *is* a bit crooked."

The cramp kept tightening. "Come here," Libby gasped. "I'll straighten it out for you."

Del prudently remained out of reach. "I don't think so. Here. Hold my hand."

Libby grabbed his hand, squeezing as the pain peaked again. She rode the wave, her fingers clenched around his. When she was done, she stared up at him, her eyes dark and exhausted. "Del, I don't think I can do this much longer."

He didn't see how she could, either. Everyone—the doctor, the labor nurses coming on and off shift—kept assuring them Libby was progressing nicely, in fact, quite rapidly for a "primip" or first-timer. Del hated to imagine how long the process must take for those not progressing quite so "nicely."

Somehow he hadn't expected it to last so long—or hurt Libby quite so much. The film they'd seen had only been half an hour, after all. A little grunting, a little sweating and the baby had slipped out. He'd expected Libby to do the same.

At first, it seemed as if that might happen. Libby had been very calm during her early contractions, much calmer than he'd felt. His stomach had felt as if it had jumped into his throat when her water burst in the garage, and he'd kept swallowing, trying to force it back down.

He'd wanted to rush her to the hospital; she'd insisted they wait. She'd taken the time to collect her overnight bag, pillow and a carefully selected set of tiny clothes for the baby. She'd even taken a shower. He'd wondered if she'd even need him, she'd been so self-possessed.

Now he was in no doubt: Libby needed him all right. If he wasn't there, who would she vent her spleen on?

"Del..."

He looked at her. Her brown eyes were suddenly vulnerable. "They're sure my slip didn't hurt the baby?"

"Positive."

"How do they know?"

Patiently he repeated what he'd already told her several times already—information the doctor and nurses had told her, too. "Because the monitor and every other indication shows that the baby is fine. They think you were probably in the first stage of labor for a couple of hours before it even happened." He frowned. "Although I still don't understand why you didn't tell me your back was hurting."

"I didn't think it meant anything," she said, responding to the faintly scolding note in his voice. "My back hurts a lot lately."

She fell silent as the labor nurse, a plump, gray-haired woman, briskly entered the room. "We're coming along," the nurse said, checking the tape the monitor steadily disgorged. She studied the series of zigzagging lines and then glanced at Del, "I can stay for a while if you want to take a short break."

Libby clutched his hand tighter. "Don't go," she said, ignoring the nurse's frown.

Del patted her hand, a feeling of warmth settling in his chest. She did want him there. "I won't," he promised.

With a disapproving cluck the nurse left. Libby

waited until the door shut behind her before confiding to Del, "She doesn't like me."

He glanced at her in surprise. "Sure she does. She seems nice."

"To *you*," Libby said. "She thinks I'm a wimp."

"Nah. I'm sure she doesn't."

Libby knew better. No wonder birthing women wanted someone to be with them during the process. They knew instinctively that labor nurses had seen the process too many times to provide much sympathy.

Another wave gathered. She gritted her teeth. Del squeezed her hand to get her attention. "Relax," he ordered. "Work with the pain—don't tense up against it."

He coached her along and Libby heaved a sigh of relief when the contraction released her again. She'd once thought she wouldn't want Del around to see her grunt, sweat and strain. During the past few hours she'd discovered intense pain won out over vanity any day. She didn't know what she'd do without the sound of his calm, patient orders. She'd been probed, pricked, cleaned up and cleaned out. She was anchored to the delivery bed by the fetal monitor strapped around her stomach and the IV attached to her wrist. And she was tired of it all.

She started to sit up.

"What is it?" Del asked sharply, his arm sliding around her shoulders to steady her. "Do you want to push?"

"No, I want to go home." Why hadn't she thought of it before? Libby wondered. If she could just get out of this white, sterile prison everything would be fine. She tried to swing her legs over the side of the bed.

Del's arm tightened. "Stop it, Libby. You aren't going anywhere."

She wanted to argue—she wanted to cry. The pain was rising again—stronger this time.

"Breathe slowly," Del demanded. "No—don't shut your eyes and grimace. Look at me."

His will was stronger than hers. She looked into his blue eyes as the pain crested, then flowed away.

When the monitor slowed its excited beeping, he dropped a kiss on her forehead. "Good job. You're doing great, sweetheart. Honestly."

The nurse bustled back in, checking the monitor and Libby. Despite her no-nonsense attitude, she was very gentle as she checked how many centimeters Libby had dilated. "Shouldn't be long now," she said, lowering the sheet and giving Libby's knee an encouraging pat before she left again.

Libby didn't believe her. Nurses had been telling her the same thing since she came in yesterday afternoon. "Oh, no, not again," she whimpered, feeling the gathering tension beneath her belly. "Del, I just can't take anymore."

But Del was relentless. She didn't want to breathe, she didn't want to concentrate, but he made her, cupping her face between his hands and holding her gaze. More people were in the room now, she noticed vaguely between the ever-quickening contractions. Her doctor—who'd made herself pretty scarce after the initial check on Libby's condition—and another doctor, who Del told her was a neonatologist, specializing in newborns.

But it didn't seem important who was there, a

marching band could have passed through for all the attention Libby paid to anyone. Her whole focus was on Del and the pains that kept intensifying until suddenly they weren't pains at all but a rippling motion that seized her body.

"She's ready," the nurse announced. "We're going to start pushing now, Libby."

Excitement built in the room. Libby could see the anticipation in the doctors' and nurses' intent faces. New energy surged through Libby. She strained and sweated, concentrating only on Del's low coaxing tones, his intent face. "Good girl," he said, helping to support her. "You can do it, Libby. It's coming. It's coming! Oh, Libby!"

Wonder suddenly crossed his face.

"The head's out," the doctor announced. "Pant through the next contraction, Libby, and then one more big push ought to do it."

She panted through the next contraction, resisting her body's urgings, then bore down, straining with all her might. Her insides seemed to drop as the baby whooshed out.

"It's a girl!"

"My God, she's a miracle." Moisture gleamed in Del's eyes and his arm tightened around Libby's shoulders. "Look, Libby. We made a real, little person."

Weariness forgotten, Libby reached eagerly for her baby. But the neonatologist and a nurse had taken her away to a draped table across the room. They were working intently over the small, purplish body.

Fear gripped Libby. "What's wrong?" The baby

hadn't cried, she realized suddenly. "Del! Please go see what's happening!"

But he was already instinctively moving in that direction, his face tense.

The labor nurse stepped up to Libby's side. She took Libby's hand in a comforting grip.

Oh, please let my baby be all right, Libby prayed silently. *Please cry, darling!*

Come on little one, you can do it, Del urged silently. The baby looked so still and lifeless in the doctor's hands.

Suddenly the small body arched. Tiny lungs filled and a quivering wail pierced the air.

Joyous tears filled Libby's eyes. The nurse patted her hand. "There. See, she's just fine. They're cleaning her up and handing her to your husband right now to bring to you."

Del took the blanketed bundle in his arms...and fell in love. He could actually feel his heart melting at the sight of those pansy eyes, button nose and pink dab of a mouth. Her skin had pinkened and the dark tuft of hair on her head stood straight up. Her fingers were so tiny. And her toes! He hesitantly touched a small foot. Had any baby anywhere ever had such exquisitely formed feet? She looked like a doll, and yet she felt so alive in his arms as she stretched her little arms and tried to kick her legs.

He walked back to Libby as carefully as if he were carrying a load of dynamite that could go off at any minute, his eyes fixed on the baby's face. Her mouth opened, revealing a miniature tongue. So sweet, so alive—yet so alarming was the cry she gave that he handed her to Libby in anxious relief.

For a moment, Libby couldn't see her daughter clearly. Tears still blinded her. She blinked the wetness away, half laughing with delight at the feel of the warm little body in her arms. Slowly, the small face came into focus. The baby—her very own baby—had her daddy's dark hair, his blue eyes. Surely there was some resemblance to herself in that puckered pink mouth? And that nose—where had she gotten such a tiny, adorable button of a nose?

"Isn't she beautiful?" Del asked, leaning closer to nudge a small fist with his finger. "Her head's a little pointy—but we can always put a hat on her."

"Her head's not pointy!" Libby protested.

"She's a bit scrawny, too."

"She's *petite!*"

"She's perfect," said the labor nurse, giving Del a reproving look. "A lot of newborns' heads look like that for a day or so after they're born." She smiled down at Libby. "She's wonderful. You did a great job."

Libby smiled back. "Thanks."

With a final pat on Libby's shoulder, the woman walked toward the door. When she opened it, a wail could be heard from down the hall.

"You stupid, selfish jerk! If you ever so much as look at me again, I'm going to—"

The door slammed shut.

"Looks like another mother-to-be just came in," Del noted.

Libby pursed her lips in disapproval. "There's no

need for all that screaming. You'd think the woman would try to control herself.''

He grinned. "Yeah. You'd think so."

He watched Libby fuss with the blanket and cuddle the baby close. She checked fingers and toes, and the ID bracelet on the baby's wrist that was a small duplicate of her own. She kissed a tiny plump cheek and the baby turned, seeking blindly with her mouth.

Del stared at the two of them. They were so involved in each other. Some of his joy faded. He felt like an interloper...but he couldn't tear himself away. "What are you going to name her, Libby?"

"I'm not sure..."

"What about Nikki?" he asked almost diffidently. "After your Dad."

Something in his voice caught Libby's attention. She glanced up. He looked tired, almost as tired as she felt, but for once his thoughts weren't hidden. His lean face was soft with yearning tenderness as he stared down at the baby in her arms.

Libby's heart, full to bursting already, ached a little more as she nestled the soft bundle closer. Nikki. Yes, she looked like a Nikki.

Del added, "And maybe Elizabeth for a middle name? After you and your mom?"

"I think that's a wonderful idea," she choked out. Wanting to touch him, she reached up and put her hand on his arm.

Immediately, Del sank down beside her on the bed, a smile curving his mouth. He put his arm around her shoulders, and rested his chin on her hair as he gazed down at his daughter.

Libby leaned back against his strong chest, savoring the sense of completeness she felt whenever he was near. She had him at her side, her baby in her arms. The happiness rushing through her was almost unbearable.

She looked up into the understanding blue eyes above her. "Oh, Del," she choked out. "You'll never know how *much* I wanted a girl!"

14

——➤ ◀——

For the next two days Libby was the happiest woman in the state, in the country, in the whole world. Del stayed almost constantly by her side, and Libby smiled almost continually, enjoying the sense of being a family. She never ceased to be amazed by her small daughter. Nikki's expressions, her sounds, her movements—all were miraculous and new. And her heart filled with tenderness whenever she watched Del with his little daughter as he changed a tiny diaper or carefully wrapped Nikki up. Life was absolutely perfect.

On the last morning before Del arrived, the nurse handed Libby a form. "It's for the birth certificate," the nurse explained. "Fill it out and leave it at the desk before you check out today."

Lying in the hospital bed, Libby stared at the form for a long time before laying it down and picking back up the birth announcement she'd been trying to fill out. She nibbled her pen, studying the blanks on the pink card. The baby's weight was no problem. Nikki had weighed in at a solid six pounds, four ounces. Libby jotted down Nikki's length, too—an impressive eighteen inches. The date and time were easy. Nikki had made her appearance on October 19, at precisely 8:00 a.m.

No, it was the blank for the name that made Libby pause. Nicole Elizabeth…Sinclair. That sounded pretty. Nicole Elizabeth Delaney. That sounded even better.

Libby chewed on her pen again. Del would certainly think so…wouldn't he? But if so, then why hadn't he mentioned marriage again? He'd certainly been all for it a few weeks ago. Could he have changed his mind?

Of course not. She didn't doubt he loved the baby. There was too much tenderness in his face when he looked at her for there to be any question on that score. And surely now that Nikki was here, he could see how important it was to be with a child every day. Why, already she was changing. She'd lost the pointy-headed look, for one thing.

He was probably just waiting for the right time to ask Libby to marry him again.

She hastily shoved all the papers under the covers when he suddenly appeared at the door. "Hey, aren't my girls ready to go yet?" he asked, heading directly for Nikki's bassinet next to the bed. He smiled down at his daughter, saying over his shoulder to Libby, "I thought you were ready to blow this joint."

"I am," Libby answered. "Nikki's all ready. Would you mind taking her for a little walk or something while I get dressed and take a shower?"

"Sure." He reached down and wrapped Nikki up in a receiving blanket, nice and tight like a little mummy. Not even Libby could do a wrap job like he could, he thought proudly.

He scooped her up, cradling her head in his hand and tucking her body along his arm like a football.

"We'll be back in about half an hour," he told Libby and strode out into the corridor.

Not much going on here, he decided, looking up and down the empty hall. He glanced down into the baby's face. "Wanna go see some other babies?" he asked.

He took Nikki over to the nursery window. Five or so babies were lined up in baskets—like loaves of bread in a bakery window, Del thought indulgently. "So, what do you think of the other kids? All kinds of babies here. Little ones, big ones— Whoa! Get a load of that chunky one in the corner!" He held Nikki up a little so she could see.

Nikki yawned.

"Not interested, huh?" Del nuzzled her swatch of hair, shutting his eyes to take a deep breath. She smelled like baby powder and milk. He gently dropped a kiss on her little head.

"Why, hello. You're here, too?" someone asked from behind him.

Del turned around. Ken was standing there, beaming at him. "Looks like we both graduated from class early," Ken said, noticing the baby in Del's arm. "There's my son, Kenneth, Jr., right there." He proudly pointed through the window at the chubby, blond baby that seemed to almost fill the whole bassinet.

Kind of a plain little guy, Del thought, politely checking him out. "He looks just like you," he told Ken.

Ken smiled smugly. "We think so. And who's that?"

Happy to show Ken what a baby *should* look like, Del pulled back the blanket to display his daughter's face. "This is Nicole Elizabeth," he said proudly. "I named her."

Ken regarded her rather doubtfully. "She's...nice. But isn't she a bit undersized?"

"She's *petite*."

"Oh." Ken glanced at his son again, adding in satisfaction, "Yeah, well, not Kenneth. He weighed in at ten pounds, five ounces."

Del gave a low whistle. "Barbie must have enjoyed that."

Ken stiffened. "She handled herself with... decorum."

"Yeah," Del answered. "Libby, too. We heard Barbie come in. Nikki was already here by then, of course. She came through the gate at 8:00 a.m." He paused. "When did junior clock in?"

"Eleven something," Ken admitted.

Del smiled in satisfaction. "Looks like we were the first to deliver. Well, we have to get going. See you later, Ken...Kip."

"You, too, Del...Ned."

Del paused. "Ned?"

Ken took off his glasses to polish them. "Sure. Her initials are N.E.D., aren't they? Your last name *is* Delaney, isn't it?"

"Yeah," Del agreed. But *Libby's* wasn't. Still, after all they'd been through together, she'd be bound to give Nikki his name...wouldn't she?

"Talk to you later," he said abruptly. With a nod in Ken's direction, he headed back toward Libby's room, his scowl deepening. His expression darkened even more when he noticed the tag on Nikki's wrist. Around a corner and out of sight of the nursery, he stopped to check it. *Sinclair*. Damn it, Libby had put Sinclair on *his* baby.

Libby looked up as he strode into the room. She was dressed in a yellow blouse he'd never seen before and her blue maternity pants. She said, ruefully, "I couldn't get into my regular pants, but at least this blouse fits." Self-consciously, she fingered the buttons straining across her breasts, smiling almost shyly up at him. Her smile faded, however, when she caught sight of his expression. "What's wrong? Is it the baby?" She reached out automatically for her daughter.

"No—well, sort of," he said, relinquishing Nikki. When Libby's gaze shot to his in alarm, he amended, "What I mean is—damn it, Libby, will you marry me?"

Her eyes widened with surprise. "Why...Del. Are you sure?"

"Of course I'm sure. I want Nikki—and you—to have my name. I want you to be my wife. I want everyone to know—" especially other men, he added silently "—that we're a family. So will you do it?"

Her brown eyes softened. Her smile glowed. "Yes."

He caught her in his arms for a deep kiss, careful not to crush Nikki between them. When he finished, he held Libby gently by the shoulders, saying, "I'll call city hall. Maybe we can do the deed tomorrow—"

"No, let's wait and have a church ceremony next week," Libby said excitedly. "I want Chris to be there—and maybe my mother... What wrong?"

Del was shaking his head.

Her brow wrinkled in confusion. "You don't want a church ceremony?"

"We don't have time for one. I have to be in Hawaii by Thursday to board a MAC flight."

Her eyes widened in bewilderment. "But you can't. You asked me to marry you...I thought you'd decided to stay."

"I can't stay, Libby. I'll lose my promotion if don't return." He put his hand on her arm. "But I'll be back..."

She moved away and his hand dropped. Libby's eyes were wet, but her chin lifted and her mouth firmed as she asked, "When? Next week?"

He slowly shook his head.

"Next month? Next year?" She stared at him with angry eyes. "You still want it all your own way, don't you, Del? Well, I'm sorry but I'm going to have to decline your flattering offer."

His face darkened. "Nicole's my daughter, too, Libby, and whether you like it or not you're going to have to admit it. I'll take the matter to court if I have to."

The baby started crying, startled perhaps by the harshness in his voice. Libby glanced away without answering, patting her daughter soothingly. She swallowed, trying to force down the lump lodged in her throat and bent to pick up the baby bag.

A stack of pink cards, tucked underneath, slid off the bed and onto the floor.

Del picked one up, automatically scanning the information she'd printed inside. The name Nicole Elizabeth Delaney leapt up at him.

His astonished gaze lifted to Libby's. She smiled without humor. "Don't worry. I'd already decided it was stupid not to admit the truth. The few times a year you're home, you'll have your daughter."

"Libby..." Arms outstretched he took a step toward her.

She stepped back. "But you won't have me."

She wouldn't speak to him after that. Nothing beyond the barest necessities. She ignored him all the way home, and once there, Libby barricaded herself behind the baby, Christine and a steady stream of visiting women.

Del kept waiting for Libby to relent. Surely she'd settle this before he left. She had to realize there was nothing else he could do. Libby would change her mind. He was so sure of it that when footsteps crunched across the graveled driveway early the next morning as he was getting the truck ready to drive to the airport, he turned, expecting to see her.

For a moment, in the hazy dawn light, he thought the small, brown-hooded figure was Libby and his heart jumped in hope. Then she spoke, and he realized it was Dorrie Jean.

"Hello, Del," she said. "Are you leaving again already?"

There was no accusation in her tone, but for some reason the question made him feel slightly defensive. "I've been here almost a month," he said. Turning away, he resumed wiping the ice off the windshield. "What are you doing up so early?"

Her breath misted out like smoke as she replied, "I'm usually up at this time. I like to take walks when no one is around."

Del grunted, not really interested in Dorrie Jean's morning habits. Although the glass was clear now, he kept wiping, sending a glance toward his house. If Libby was going to come out, she should do it any minute, he thought. She'd come out the last time to say goodbye.

As if she could read his thoughts, Dorrie said suddenly, "I saw you leave after the blizzard, you know. When Libby came out to help you shovel out the truck."

Del paused, turning to look at his neighbor. Dorrie Jean was watching him solemnly, her hands thrust deep into her coat pockets, her shoulders hunched against the cold.

"You knew I was here?"

She nodded. "I figured you were probably the father of the baby."

He gave the glass a couple more swipes. "So why didn't you say anything?"

"It was none of my business. Just like it's none of my business that you're leaving again."

He slanted her a sardonic look. "But you think I'm being unfair to Libby."

To his surprise, she shook her head. "No, I think if you want to go, you should. Libby will do fine without you."

It was what he'd thought, too, but somehow when she put it into words, he didn't quite like the idea. "Christine will help her," he said, as if she had argued. "And I know you will, too."

Dorrie Jean nodded. "Yes. Everyone cares about Libby—she wants so much for people to like her. And Nicole is darling. You won't need to worry about them being lonely."

"Good," he said shortly. He scrubbed harder. "I'm providing for her financially, you know," he said.

Dorrie Jean nodded, looking thoughtful. "That's nice...but I don't think Libby is looking for financial support. What she needs is more emotional. She hasn't been as spoiled as you.''

Spoiled? Del straightened, intending to ask Dorrie what the hell she meant by that, but before he could, she glanced at her house, saying, ''Uh-oh. The kitchen light is on. Mother is going to wonder where I am.''

She strode off, calling over her shoulder, ''Bye, Del. See you whenever you get back.''

He watched until she disappeared into her house, then glanced at his own. No lights were on there. Each window yawned dark and silent.

Libby wasn't coming out.

He threw the wet cloth onto the floor in the back seat. Fine, he couldn't wait any longer for her, anyway. He'd have a hard time catching his plane as it was.

Yet when he started the truck and backed out of the driveway, he couldn't stop himself from looking back one last time. Never before had he felt so reluctant to leave home. In the past, he'd been focused on where he was going, not on what he was leaving behind. Yet, he couldn't get his mind off Libby.

Of course she would do fine without him. She had the last time... He frowned. Or had she? She'd been pregnant the last time he'd left. And she'd never even called to let him know.

Still, this time she'd do okay. Like Dorrie Jean said, everyone liked Libby. Christine, Mrs. Peyton, Susan...that damn doctor. He scowled. Hopefully, *he* wouldn't be coming around, but still...what was there to stop him? Libby wasn't married, after all. And Dorrie Jean claimed she was looking for—what was it she'd called it? Emotional support? Whatever the hell that meant?

And why had she called him spoiled? Libby's mother had been the one with money. He'd come from a middle-class family with old-fashioned values. His parents had taught both him and Chris that, with hard work and perseverance, they could achieve whatever they set out to do. And he had. Why else would he be flying off now to the ends of the earth to meet the obligations of his well-paying job?

He reached the Portland airport and went through the boarding process almost automatically, still trying to figure out what Dorrie Jean had meant. It wasn't until he was on the commercial three-hour flight to Hawaii that he really became aware of his surroundings again.

A baby's cry brought him out of his abstraction. Across the aisle, a young mother was trying to quiet her fussy infant. The sounds reminded him of Nikki, and his heart seemed to tighten. How was *his* baby doing? She'd be okay with her mother, of course—but what about when Libby was really tired? He knew how to get Nikki to sleep. She really liked it when he stroked her temple with his finger and thumb, down the sides of her little face to her chin. Her blue eyes would widen, and gradually drift shut.

He shifted restlessly in his seat. He'd never told Libby about that little trick...and he should have. She might need to try it sometime when the baby refused to be soothed.

Like the baby across the aisle. The poor little thing was really gearing up now. No one else seemed to be bothered. The chubby man next to him was snoring, and up ahead a blond woman with the pinched-face look of a professional model didn't even look up from her fashion magazine.

But the baby's pitiful wailing made Del long to do something. He leaned over to offer his help. The young mother glanced up at him with so much suspicion in her tired eyes that he changed his mind. He couldn't blame her for being wary. He was a stranger. He wouldn't want Libby to give Nikki to someone she didn't know or trust, either.

"Sorry, I didn't mean to startle you," he found himself explaining. "I just left my own newborn. Nikki hasn't quite figured out an appropriate schedule yet, either."

The woman gently bounced the baby against her shoulder, giving him a weary smile. "You must miss her."

"I do," Del admitted, realizing the truth of the statement. He'd only been away for an hour and he already missed her like crazy. Missed both of them.

The woman sighed. "I bet your wife is lonely for you, too."

Del thought of the dark house, the empty driveway, the tearful goodbye that had never happened. "Actually, I think they're getting along just fine without me."

She smiled wryly. "I wouldn't count on it. It's so hard to take care of a baby all alone. It's easier when you're with someone who cares about you…" She bit her lip, as if conscious of revealing too much to a casual stranger, before leaning back against the headrest, shutting her eyes with another sigh.

The baby finally stopped crying. Del should have felt better, but instead a yawning emptiness grew in his stomach. Because all at once, he understood what Dorrie Jean had been trying to tell him. Financially and physically, Libby could raise Nikki on her own.

That wasn't what she wanted from him. As Dorrie Jean and the stranger across the aisle had implied, what Libby needed was someone to be there through the emotional ups and downs of everyday life. Someone to help her make the little and big decisions that would affect their child. Someone who loved them both with all his heart. Someone like him.

He grimaced. Dorrie Jean had been right about something else. He *was* spoiled. Because of his parents' solid marriage, he'd always known love existed, that it was waiting out there for him to claim...when *he* was ready. In *his* time. When it didn't interfere with his goals and ambitions.

So when he'd met Libby and fallen in love with her in three short days, he'd refused to admit what had happened. It would upset all his plans, his ambitions. It wasn't convenient right now. So he'd entered into an affair with her, telling himself it was only a temporary arrangement—when he'd known deep inside that his feelings for her hadn't been temporary at all.

But much worse than his self-deception was that he'd taken advantage of Libby. She hadn't had the security of a normal background with two loving parents. That had been evident by her interest in the stories he'd shared about his family, the hunger in her face as she'd listened. But he'd wooed and seduced her, letting the yearning in her heart for a family overcome her skittishness at his touch, coaxing her into accepting him, knowing that the act of making love would bind her to him more surely—and with less trouble on his part—than a ring ever would.

Oh, it sounded good—to say how could he have known she was a virgin when she hadn't told him so— but from her tiny gasp, the surprise in her eyes the first time he'd touched her intimately, he'd known that if she wasn't a virgin, she was inexperienced enough that it made no difference.

So he hadn't been surprised to feel the small barrier of her innocence—in fact, the realization as he'd entered her tight, clinging body had filled him with a fierce, primitive possessiveness. She was his and his alone.

But selfishly, he hadn't wanted to admit that he also belonged to her. He'd grown used to his freedom, his hedonistic existence where the only relationship he had was the nondemanding one with his sister, which didn't restrict him in any way. He'd grown used to only considering himself.

So he'd left, making sure before he'd done so that Libby was bound to the relationship. He'd told her he'd be back, making the arrogant assumption that since they were consenting adults, a once-or-twice-a-year love affair would suit them both. But deep inside he'd known, when she hadn't called, that it didn't suit her—that it never would.

Across the way, the baby started whimpering. The man next to him continued to snore. Del looked past him to gaze out the window, mentally counting the miles and miles of vast ocean that lay between him and his family.

You picked a fine time, Delaney, he told himself, *to realize what a pigheaded fool you've been.*

How was it, Libby wondered the next morning, that a house could be full of people, yet feel so empty?

With Nikki nestled on her shoulder, Libby smiled and talked with Mrs. Peyton and Dorrie Jean, both of whom had stopped by for a visit. Yet she constantly found herself listening for someone who wasn't there.

Which was stupid of her. What had she expected? That he would change his mind and stay home, after all? Of course he wouldn't.

Still when the front door opened unexpectedly in the middle of Mrs. P.'s latest saga about her rheumatism, Libby's heart leapt with hope—only to fall again as Christine came in.

Libby forced a smile at her friend.

Christine smiled back. "I picked up all the groceries you'll need—enough to last at least a week or two, Libby." Her smile faded and a small frown puckered her brow. "I'm sorry I have to leave so soon again. Are you sure you'll be okay?"

"Of course, I will. I just had a baby—that doesn't make me an invalid. Nikki and I will do just fine," Libby said.

"Don't you worry," Mrs. Peyton added, "I'll stop by daily in case Libby needs anything."

"Me, too," said Dorrie Jean quietly.

Libby smiled at them. "Thank you," she said gratefully. They were so sweet. And what an idiot she was to be thinking that she only wanted Del.

The tears that had been threatening since she heard his truck leave yesterday at dawn burned behind her eyes, but Libby fiercely refused to let them fall. *You survived the last time he left*, she reminded herself, *and you'll do so again.* She was simply having a case of the baby blues. And expecting Del to walk in the door at any moment certainly wasn't helping.

Maybe it wasn't a good idea to stay here—where everything constantly reminded her of him. Maybe she should move somewhere else.

Nikki, as if sensing her mother's distress, wriggled restlessly and uttered a short wail. Mrs. Peyton pounced. "She can't be hungry again!" the older woman exclaimed.

"I don't think so," Libby said. She certainly hoped not. Her nipples were so sore. Her daughter might be tiny, but she nursed like a starving piglet. "She just ate half an hour ago."

"She's gassy," Mrs. P. decided. "I can tell the signs. Why don't you give her to me, Libby? I'll burp her again for you."

A bit reluctantly, Libby handed the baby over.

The older woman cooed in Nikki's face. The baby stopped crying. "She likes me!" Mrs. P. announced triumphantly. "I told you I'm good with babies. She's stopped fussing."

"She's probably startled at hearing a strange voice," Christine suggested, bringing in a plate of cookies.

Mrs. Peyton glared at her. "Nonsense. She probably thinks that I'm her grandmother." She lifted the baby to her shoulder and patted her soothingly on the back, asking, "What did your mother say about her, Libby?"

"I haven't told her yet," Libby admitted without thinking.

She immediately wished she hadn't. Mrs. Peyton looked aghast. "Libby! A girl's mother should be the first to know."

No, the father should, Libby thought, remembering the wonder on Del's face when he'd first seen his daughter.

"You'd better tell her right away," Mrs. P. declared. "Go on and call her now, if you like. I'll take care of Nikki,'' she added in a blatant attempt to hold the baby awhile longer.

Libby didn't argue. Suddenly she wanted to call her mother. Perhaps she should see about going home.

She excused herself and went into the study. Del's computer was there. She turned her back to the blank screen as she dialed her mother's number.

For once she didn't have to wait the required fifteen minutes. Liz came to the phone immediately. ''It's about time you called,'' she said. ''I've been waiting to hear from you. It wasn't until I'd gotten off the line the last time that I realized I'd forgotten to get your number at that godforsaken place.''

''I'll give it to you in a minute,'' Libby promised. She twisted the cord around her finger. ''But what I really called to tell you is that I had the baby.''

The silence at the other end of the line stretched for a full ten seconds. ''I'm speechless,'' Liz finally declared. ''That has to have been the shortest pregnancy on record. I get a call to tell me you're pregnant and a few weeks later, you've had the baby.''

''I was already almost full-term,'' Libby said, stating the obvious.

''Are you all right?'' Liz's voice held a familiar peevish note. Obviously she didn't appreciate her daughter's tardy revelations.

''I'm fine—and so is the baby. It's a girl. We—I named her Nicole, after Dad, and Elizabeth, after you.''

''Why, Libby, that's so sweet.'' Genuine pleasure rang in her mother's voice. Then she added more prosaically, ''Of course, Elizabeth Nicole might be even better...''

A reluctant smile curved Libby's lips. Trust Liz to

think of something like that. "I think two women with the first name of Elizabeth are enough for one family," she said gently.

Liz sighed. "Well, it's your decision—and the father's, I suppose. Is he still around?"

Libby gripped the phone a little tighter, the unexpected question causing a tightness in her throat. "No," she said huskily.

Another silence. "Darling, I'm so sorry. So I guess he didn't propose."

"Oh, he proposed. I said no."

"But why?"

"Because he wasn't going to stay around. His job involves traveling about ten months a year."

"Oh, darling, that's so sad. He should have told you."

Libby frowned, fiddling with the phone cord. "Actually, he did tell me about it."

"*After* you became involved."

Libby shifted uneasily. "Well, no. He told me before."

"Oh." If for a moment Liz sounded nonplussed, she recovered quickly. "Well, he should have given up his job," she declared stoutly. "He should have stayed with you and the baby. Men can be so selfish."

She then launched into a recital of the events in her own life. Libby barely listened, shifting uneasily again. She'd thought the same thing about Del. Yet, somehow it sounded different when Liz said it. She interrupted her mother's monologue on her newest movie role. "He's not really selfish, Mother," she felt compelled to explain. "He stayed as long as he could. He was here for the birth, in fact. And he's providing for us financially."

But Liz had lost interest in the unknown father. "That's the least he should do. Anyway," she added briskly, "when are you coming home? I can't wait to see my namesake."

She'd planned to go home when she'd picked up the phone—but now Libby wasn't sure that was the answer. "I don't know," she said hesitantly. "Nikki's a little young to be traveling."

"Just let me know when you decide. And don't take too long, darling. I...I miss you."

Libby hung up the phone, confused emotions roiling inside her. She heard a noise at the door and glanced up. Dorrie Jean was standing there, holding a fussing Nikki in her arms. "I didn't mean to interrupt," Dorrie said apologetically, "but I thought I'd better take Nikki from Mom. She's getting irritable with hunger."

"But she just ate less than an hour ago!" Libby said, taking her baby.

Dorrie looked surprised. "Oh, I didn't mean Nikki—Mother's the one who's ready for lunch."

Both women looked at each other a moment, then Dorrie Jean smiled—a surprisingly rueful grin. "Mothers can be such a pain."

"You're so right," Libby agreed wryly, thinking of Liz.

"But we still love them," Dorrie added. "After all, nobody's perfect." With a small pat on Nikki's leg, she left the room.

Libby remained in the study, rocking her baby in her arms. Dorrie was right—Liz could be a pain. Their relationship wasn't the closest, nor did they often agree. She often became annoyed or hurt by Liz's theatrics, and the make-believe world her mother perpetuated frustrated her no end. But still, when all was said and done, she loved her mother, and knew that in her own way Liz loved her, too.

And maybe Liz wasn't the only Sinclair who expected to have everything her way—who expected everyone to be perfect. Libby shifted uneasily, thinking about their conversation. Had she really expected Del to give up his job, just because she wanted him to? She squirmed a little. He loved his work. Besides, Del didn't have the luxury of a mother to run home to. He'd been taking care of himself—and for a while his mother and Christine—since he was sixteen years old.

It wasn't his fault that Libby hadn't listened to him. As she'd just admitted to her mother, he'd been honest with her all along. She simply hadn't been honest with herself.

Libby winced. She'd always blamed her mother for living in an illusionary world, but hadn't she been doing the same thing? Constantly dreaming about a perfect place—with perfect people—to live in, instead of being thankful for the mother and home she had? When all was said and done, Lone Oak wasn't perfect. It was just a town—with good points and bad points— not some magical place where nothing ever went wrong. Her idea of the town had been no more real than her mother's idea of her career.

So maybe it was time to discover what *was* real in her life.

Libby frowned. Rocking the baby gently, she pondered the problem and suddenly the realization hit her. Love—that's what was real. The answer was so simple—and yet so complex. As simple as her overwhelming, protective love for the baby in her arms, and as complex as her love for the baby's father, with all the hopes, disappointments, sorrows and joys the emotion brought.

Simply because her relationship with Del hadn't been the fairy-tale romance she'd always dreamed of, she'd told herself her feelings for him didn't exist. But they did. She loved Del. She had from the first. That was the reason she hadn't moved out when he'd left. She'd known he'd be back...and she'd also known, whether she'd admitted it to herself or not, that he would never turn his back on his own child. This wonderful house somehow wasn't quite so wonderful without Del in it. It wasn't her love for the house or town that had kept her there. It was her love for him.

She sighed, cuddling the baby closer. So maybe it was time to quit playing games, time to stand on her own two feet like she kept telling Del she wanted to do. She'd move to Vicksville, or the nearby town of Cauldron. Close enough for him to see Nikki when he could, yet far enough for Libby to keep things in perspective. Because she couldn't stay here, not if he didn't love her, too. She refused to torture herself any longer with make-believe.

Nikki made a snuffling sound, beginning to whimper again. Libby pressed her lips against the baby's hair. "It's past time, sweetie," she said softly, "that your mother finally grew up."

The door opened. Libby was proud that this time she didn't hope. She didn't even glance around as she said huskily, "I think Nikki and I might be moving, Chris. Something's come up..."

The silence stretched behind her. Libby turned around to explain further and froze, her eyes widening. Del was standing in the doorway.

Del shut the door and took a step toward her, but

paused when Libby didn't move or speak. He couldn't tell what she was thinking. She looked pale and scared, staring at him with wide eyes, her hair a little messy, a towel that Nikki had burped up on thrown over her shoulder. She'd never looked more appealing…and he'd never been more afraid of losing her. He swallowed. "Please don't leave, Libby," he said. "Not right when I've come home."

She still didn't move, and his heart sank. Had he waited too long to discover what was really important in his life? "I love you," he added slowly. "I should have told you before I left—I definitely should have told you the first night we made love. Because from the moment I first saw you, I knew my life had changed."

She swallowed. "Oh, Del." Sudden tears welled in her eyes. She sniffed. "Do you mean it? You aren't just saying that to make me feel better?"

"No—but you'd sure make me feel better if you told me that you loved me, too," he said truthfully. He tried to smile, but couldn't quite manage it. "I'm dying here."

A smile trembled on her lips. "I do. You know I do."

He did know it. Her love was shining on her face in a soft glow. He strode over to her and slid his hands along her jaw into her hair, tilting her face up to his. He kissed her—long and tenderly—ignoring the indignant kicking of the baby caught between them.

Finally, he lifted his mouth. Libby sighed, relaxing against him for a moment. But Nikki was having none of that. She gave a loud wail.

Libby glanced down at her little daughter. "Oh, dear."

"'Oh, dear' is right," Del agreed, carefully taking Nikki away from her. He looked down into his baby's crumpled-up face. "Stop that," he scolded gently. "Can't you see I'm proposing to your mom?"

Abruptly, Nikki stopped crying, blinking up at him with her pansy eyes. Obviously she was as startled to see him as her mother had been. "I love you," he told Nikki, walking with her to the door, "but right now you're just a little pest. So let me find another pest to take care of you."

He opened the door. "Christine!"

"You bellowed, brother?" his sister asked, popping her head around the kitchen door.

"Yeah. Here take Nikki for a while. I need to talk with Libby." He put the baby in his sister's willing arms. He started to close the door, then paused. "Oh, and by the way…"

Christine, busy making faces at the baby, looked up inquiringly.

"…I'm Nikki's real father—and you're an aunt."

"Wah!" Chris squawked.

He shut the door in her face and locked it.

"That wasn't very nice," Libby said reprovingly, trying not to smile.

Del's smile was wide, white and satisfied. "Yeah, I know."

He strode back to Libby, anxious to have her in his arms again. He pulled her close and bent to kiss her, ignoring the pounding on the door and Christine's muffled threats.

By the time he lifted his head again, Chris had apparently given up and gone away.

Del put his lips against the soft skin of Libby's temple. "Oh, sweetheart," he breathed. "I love you so much. I never want to leave you again."

"I don't want you to." But she frowned, giving a slight push to hold him away. "But I don't want you to lose your job. I was wrong—"

"No, you were right." He hugged her to him again. "As for my work, I told them I wanted to cut back on the fieldwork—take a desk job. I may have to travel a little, but nothing like I did before."

She clutched his sleeve, her eyes troubled. "Oh, Del. Do you mind?"

He shook his head. "No. It's the work I enjoy—not the traveling. And now I have the best of both worlds. I'll be doing what I enjoy—yet will still be here with you and Nikki," he said in satisfaction. He gave her a squeeze. "I don't ever want you to get accustomed to not having me in your life."

"That would never happen." She laid her head against his shoulder. "And you're sure you want to stay in Lone Oak?"

His eyebrows lifted in surprise. "Don't you? I like this old house and town—Chris and I had a lot of fun growing up here. Can you think of a better place to raise our kids?"

She smiled mistily. "No, I can't." She held him tighter and laid her head against his shoulder. "I can't believe you're here, you want to stay—and that you love me."

"Believe it." He rocked her gently, resting his cheek against her hair. She felt so good, smelled so sweet. Like baby powder, sour milk and Libby.

She pressed a kiss against his throat, and his arms tightened around her. He could feel her smiling against his skin as she drawled, "Of course, there's one way you can make me believe it all..."

"What's that?"

"Tell me your real name."

He glanced down at her. She was watching him from beneath her lashes, a teasing smile on her face. His body tightened with desire. "Libby," he said thickly, "if you'll marry me, I'll tell the world."

Announcing the Marriage of
Elizabeth Anne Sinclair
to
Adelbertus Delaney
on Saturday, the Twenty-second of November
at the Lone Oak, Oregon, Congregational Church
"To Love and to Cherish, Forever and Ever"

* * * * *

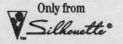

Take 4 bestselling love stories FREE

Plus get a FREE surprise gift!

Special Limited-time Offer

Mail to Silhouette Reader Service™

3010 Walden Avenue
P.O. Box 1867
Buffalo, N.Y. 14269-1867

YES! Please send me 4 free Silhouette Yours Truly™ novels and my free surprise gift. Then send me 4 brand-new novels every other month, which I will receive months before they appear in bookstores. Bill me at the low price of $2.69 each plus 25¢ delivery and applicable sales tax, if any.* That's the complete price and a savings of over 10% off the cover prices—quite a bargain! I understand that accepting the books and gift places me under no obligation ever to buy any books. I can always return a shipment and cancel at any time. Even if I never buy another book from Silhouette, the 4 free books and the surprise gift are mine to keep forever.

201 BPA AZH2

Name	(PLEASE PRINT)	
Address	Apt. No.	
City	State	Zip

This offer is limited to one order per household and not valid to present Silhouette Yours Truly™ subscribers. *Terms and prices are subject to change without notice. Sales tax applicable in N.Y.

USYRT-296   ©1996 Harlequin Enterprises Limited

As seen on TV!
Free Gift Offer

With a Free Gift proof-of-purchase from any Silhouette® book,
you can receive a beautiful cubic zirconia pendant.

This gorgeous marquise-shaped stone is a genuine cubic
zirconia—accented by an 18" gold tone necklace.

(Approximate retail value $19.95)

Send for yours today...
compliments of V *Silhouette*®

To receive your free gift, a cubic zirconia pendant, send us one original proof-of-purchase, photocopies not accepted, from the back of any Silhouette Romance™, Silhouette Desire®, Silhouette Special Edition®, Silhouette Intimate Moments® or Silhouette Yours Truly™ title available at your favorite retail outlet, together with the Free Gift Certificate, plus a check or money order for $1.65 U.S./$2.15 CAN. (do not send cash) to cover postage and handling, payable to Silhouette Free Gift Offer. We will send you the specified gift. Allow 6 to 8 weeks for delivery. Offer good until December 31, 1997, or while quantities last. Offer valid in the U.S. and Canada only.

Free Gift Certificate

Name: _____

Address: _____

City: _____ State/Province: _____ Zip/Postal Code: _____

Mail this certificate, one proof-of-purchase and a check or money order for postage and handling to: SILHOUETTE FREE GIFT OFFER 1997. In the U.S.: 3010 Walden Avenue, P.O. Box 9077, Buffalo NY 14269-9077. In Canada: P.O. Box 613, Fort Erie, Ontario L2Z 5X3.

FREE GIFT OFFER   084-KFD
ONE PROOF-OF-PURCHASE
To collect your fabulous FREE GIFT, a cubic zirconia pendant, you must include this
original proof-of-purchase for each gift with the properly completed Free Gift Certificate.

084-KFDR

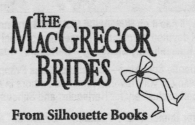